P9-CQH-980

You get **THREE GOLD STARS** for reading this book (good choice).

spare boots
Home-work
Vampire SWAMP monster
WHOOPS

mile!
Excellent Excuses
(and other good stuff)
Includes a special glossary by TOM!
By Liz Pichon
CANDLEWICK PRESS

Tree photograph on p. 21 courtesy of Lily Pichon Flannery

First U.S. edition 2015

Library of Congress Catalog Card Number 2014944793
ISBN 978-0-7636-7474-8

15 16 17 18 19 20 BVG 10 9 8 7 6 5 4 3 2 1

Printed in Berryville, VA, U.S.A.

This book was typeset in Pichon.
The illustrations were done in mixed media.

Candlewick Press
99 Dover Street
Somerville, Massachusetts 02144

visit us at www.candlewick.com

DEDICATED
to
COLIN
DAVINA
Hoagy
Nikki
Mark C.

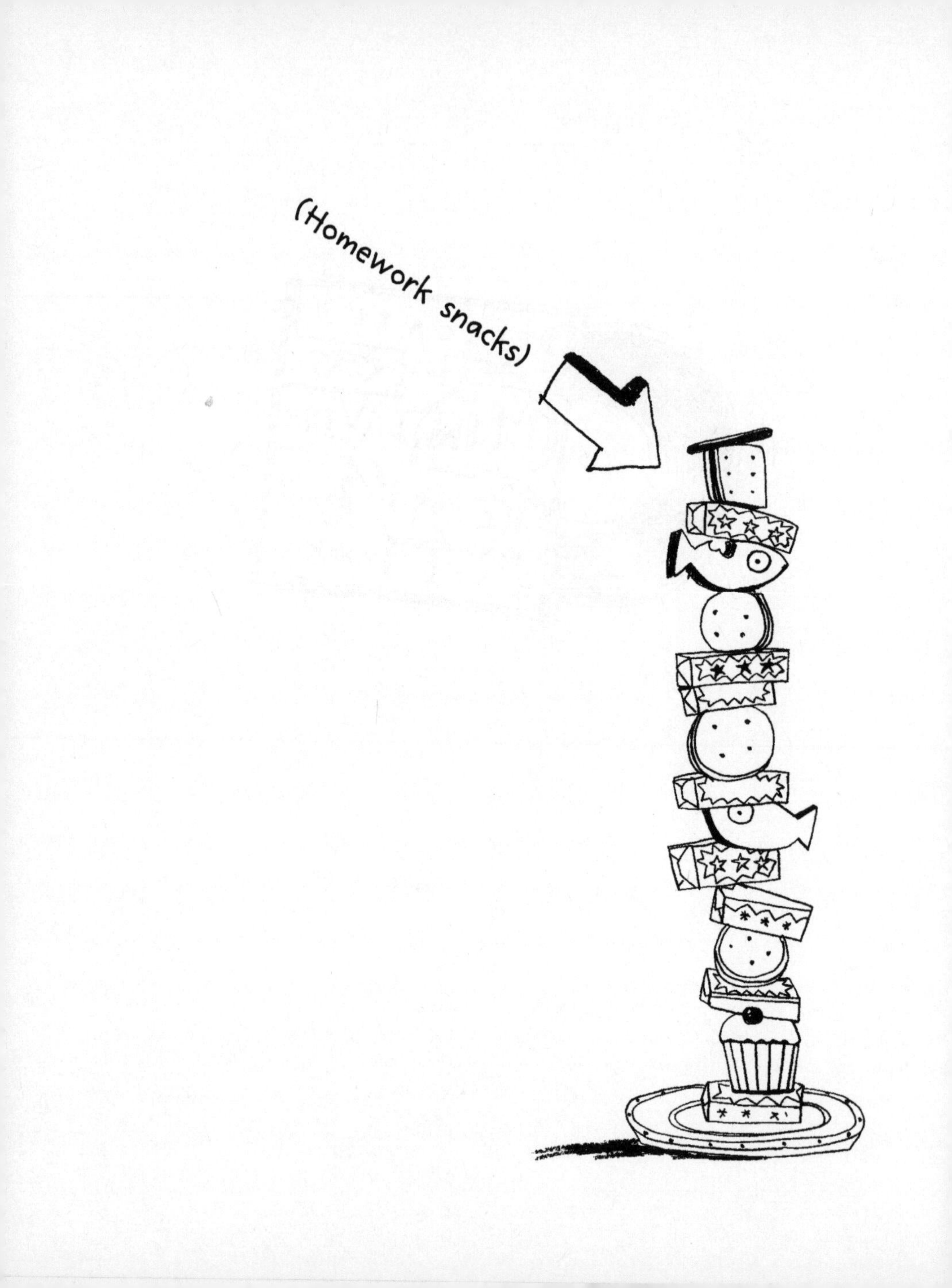
(Homework snacks)

Wake up this morning and suddenly remember something absolutely

BRILLIANT!

NO SCHOOL
FOR TWO
WHOLE
WEEKS!
Yeah!

I can forget ALL about lessons (and irritating things like Marcus Meldrew). And concentrate on GOOD stuff like:

- Inventing **new** ways to annoy my sister, Delia. (So many!)
- Drawing pictures (that annoy Delia).
- Watching TV and eating caramel wafers.
- Eating caramel wafers and watching TV.

And **most** important . . .

Band practice for
DOG ZOMBIES
with Derek
(who's my best mate and
next-door neighbor).
Tonight we're planning a sleepover
zzzzzzzzz
at his house. Which is easy to do
as he's so close.
Excellent choices.
OK!

One of the other great things about going to Derek's is he doesn't have an annoying sister (like I do) . . .

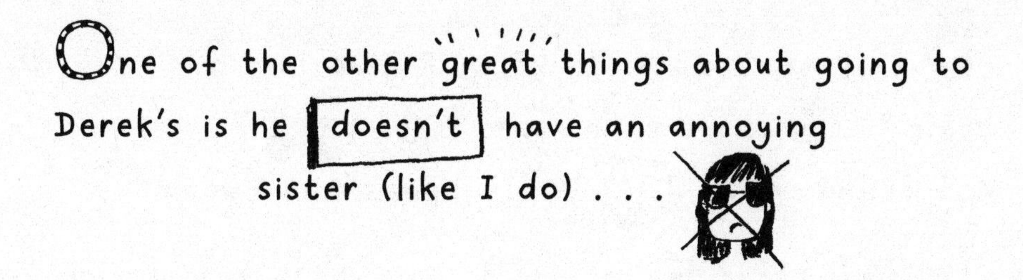

AND he has a dog called Rooster.

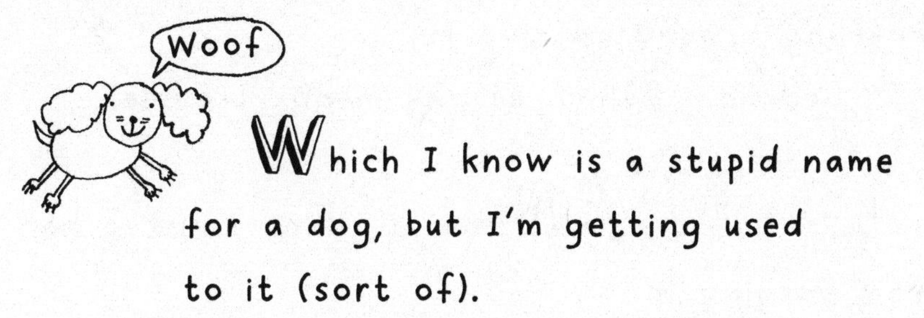

Which I know is a stupid name for a dog, but I'm getting used to it (sort of).

Sometimes, though, Rooster can be almost as annoying as Delia. Especially when he won't stop

BARKING!

Occasionally Derek throws him a Doggy Treat to shut him up.

Yum!

But if that doesn't work, I give him a pair of Delia's sunglasses to chew on. It keeps him happy for HOURS.

Right now I can hear Delia shuffling around outside my bedroom (which usually means trouble).

So I LEAN on my door to stop her from barging in.

Somehow she **still** manages to stick her **BIG** head around the door.

She says . . .

(That doesn't sound good. . . . Groan.)

I wish I could shut Delia up with a doggy treat. How good would that be?

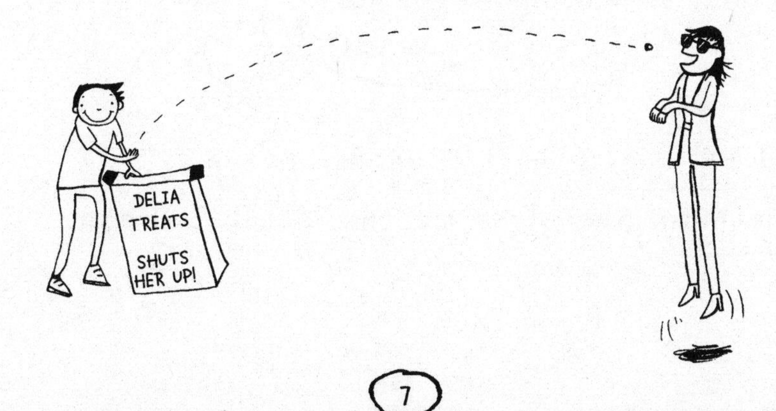

When I see Mom, she's holding a letter from school. I'm trying really hard to remember

ANYTHING I've done

that might have gotten me into trouble.

No . . . can't think of anything.

Nothing at all.

(I am innocent.)

But by the way Mom is looking at me, in that

kind of way, I must have forgotten something. She gives me the letter to read.

OK, just remembered.

To Mr. and Mrs. Gates
RE: Tom Gates Dog Attack

Dear Mr. and Mrs. Gates,

I do hope that Tom has recovered from the vicious dog that attacked him on the last day of the term as he walked to school.

What luck that he had his schoolbook to defend himself with.

I'm SO glad it was only his homework that was chewed and not Tom. Enclosed is ANOTHER copy of the HOMEWORK—to review a film/book/TV show—for Tom to complete again during his holiday.

Let's hope there are no other **ANGRY** beasts ready to pounce in the future!

Many thanks for your help.

Kind regards,

Mr. Fullerman
Class 5F Teacher

I am trying to explain to Mom what happened to me by reenacting the **whole** scene in slow motion.

(There was no choice. . . . It was me or the homework.)

But she's **not** impressed. I think she suspects I might have made up the dog attack. (I did.)

Instead I have to agree to:

1. Do my review homework (AGAIN).

2. Not use vicious dogs as an excuse for lack of homework (or any other

Grrrr

kind of creature, for that matter.)

3. Clean my room. (Mom added that one.)

Still, at

least I have

to do the

review homework in.

Though I will probably leave it until the last possible moment, like the night before school. That works for me.

"NOW?

What do you mean I have to do my homework right now? I've still got

TWO WHOLE WEEKS!"

Mom says, "There's no time like the present." Then she adds, "No sleepover at Derek's until you've done your homework."

Which is a

I **have** to think of something to review quickly. Mmmmmmmmm.

Think . . .  think . . . think . . . think . . . think. . . .

If I don't think of something FAST Mom will keep me in the house

FOREVER. Then, just to add to the

PRESSURE, Derek phones up to find out what time I'm coming over for the sleepover and band practice.

when

I hear Mom saying,

That all depends on how long it takes Tom to do his review homework, Derek.

(That's ALL I need.)

Mom thinks I should go to my room to "sit quietly and concentrate on getting it done."

(It's not working.)

So I do some drawing instead.

It's a lot more fun inventing my own characters. . . .

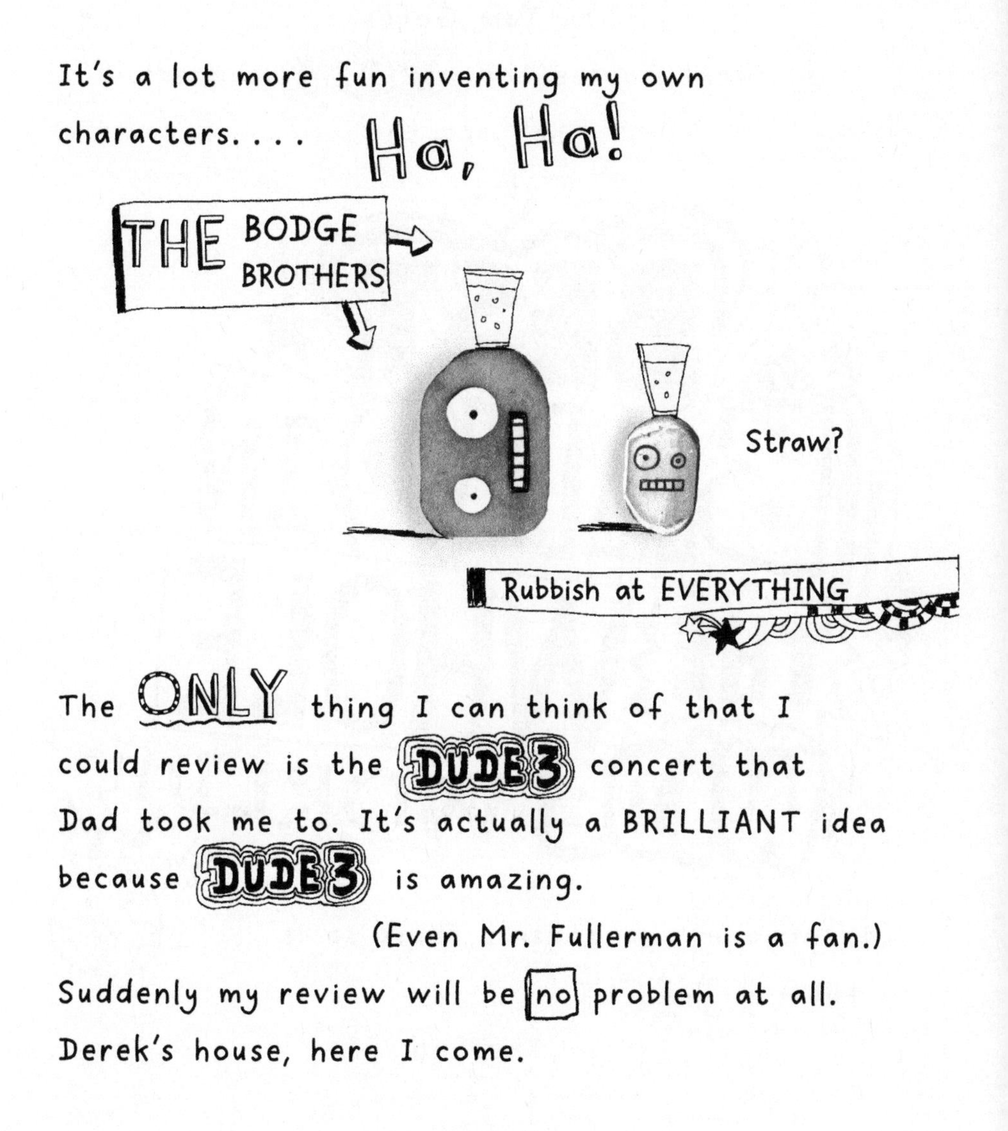

The ONLY thing I can think of that I could review is the DUDE3 concert that Dad took me to. It's actually a BRILLIANT idea because DUDE3 is amazing.

(Even Mr. Fullerman is a fan.)

Suddenly my review will be no problem at all. Derek's house, here I come.

REVIEW HOMEWORK
by Tom Gates
I went to see the DUDE 3 concert.
They are the
BEST
BAND IN
THE WHOLE
WIDE WORLD
and anyone who doesn't think so is
a total IDIOT.
The End

I run downstairs and show it quickly to Mom.

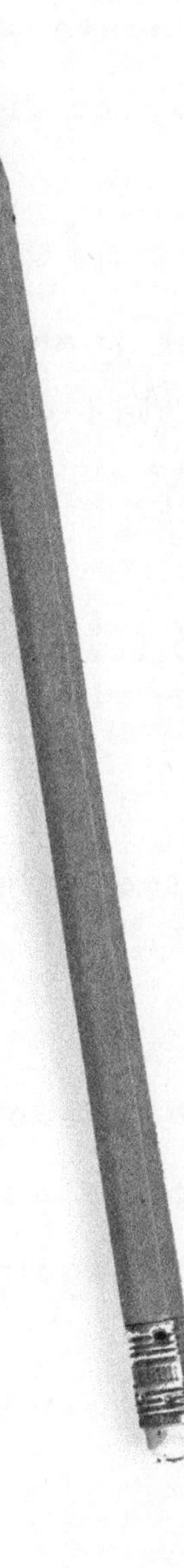

There . . . all done.

I am busy packing a few essentials for Derek's house when Dad comes up to see me.

Apparently Mom doesn't think I am taking my review homework "seriously." Dad says I have do it again "PROPERLY."

Which is a bit **HARSH**. (OK, I admit my review was short, but true.)

Dad suddenly holds up a packet of wafers.

"For the sleepover, when you've done your homework again, OK?"

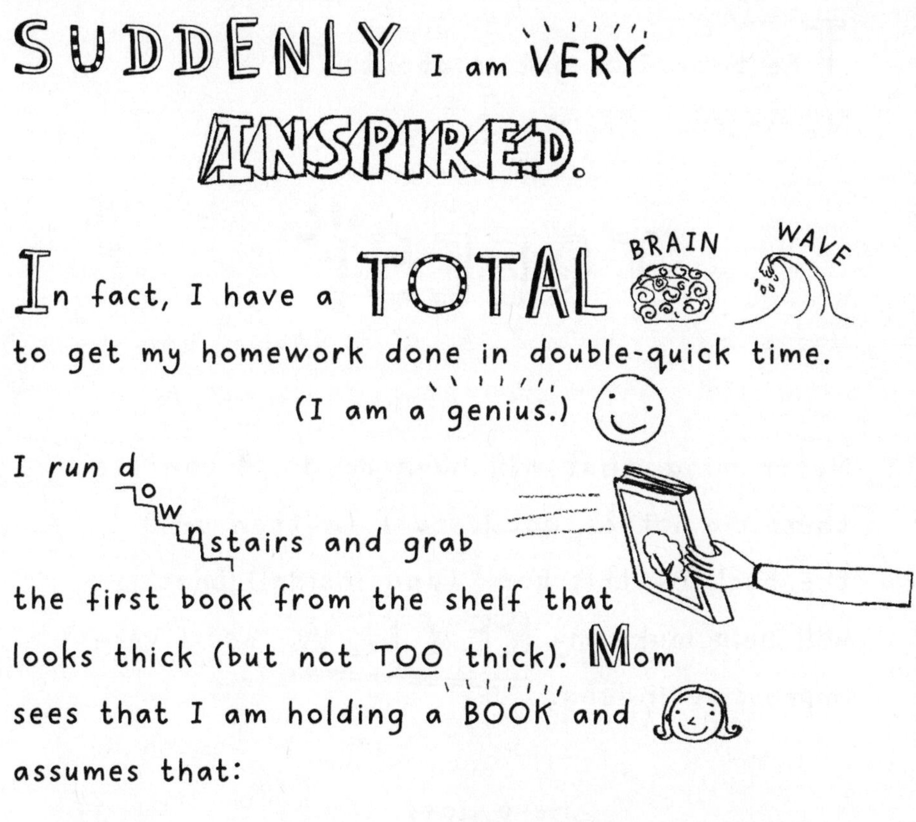

SUDDENLY I am VERY INSPIRED.

In fact, I have a TOTAL BRAIN WAVE to get my homework done in double-quick time.

(I am a genius.)

I run downstairs and grab the first book from the shelf that looks thick (but not TOO thick). Mom sees that I am holding a BOOK and assumes that:

(She looks pleased with me.)

The book I've got is about . . .
let me see . . .

TREES!

Never mind, that will have to do. I can see there's a lot of good stuff written on the back of this book (and inside!) that will help make my REVIEW seem very impressive indeed.

Here goes.

A GUIDE TO
TREES
By A. Corn

Homework FINISHED.

I tell Mom and Dad, and they want me to READ it to them.

"Yes, Tom, now. We'd love to hear it."

(Which actually means "just checking you've really done it this time.")

Delia is lurking in the kitchen, trying to listen. So I shut the kitchen door (in her face), then read it as quickly as I can.

LUCKILY, my homework is EXCELLENT (if I do say so myself).

Mom and Dad are pleased and slightly surprised I've managed to write **such** a good review SO quickly. I let them see it by *WAFTING* it under their noses . . . super fast.

(Must remember to hide the book on trees.)

Mom and Dad say well done for being so FOCUSED.

I say, "It's all due to

(Which is something I've heard my teachers say.) Then I add, "I'm actually VERY interested in TREES." (I'm not.)

SO SWEET

This goes down really well and stops Mom and Dad from asking me any more difficult questions.

GREAT!

(I should say nice stuff like that more often.)

They are both in a good mood now, so I suggest that another sign of

GOOD PARENTING

would be to reward my hard work and EFFORT with some

EXTRA

pocket money?

Which doesn't go down quite so well.

(Worth a try, though.)

Derek is happy

I've brought SNACKS.

But, stupidly, I've forgotten to bring my guitar for band practice. And far more important, I've left my special teddy at home. (I don't tell Derek because we agreed that Special Teddies were probably a bit TOO babyish now that we're in a band.)

Luckily, Derek's house is right next door to mine. So I run back home to get them both.

Delia  is sitting in the front garden with her "dodgy" boyfriend, Ed (or Ted or whatever his name is). He says, All right, Tom? (Which is nice and takes me by surprise.) Then Delia shouts,

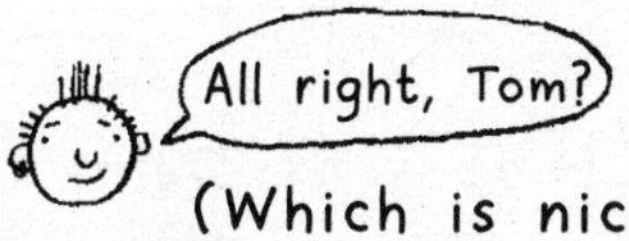

Get lost... idiot.

(Which is not a surprise at all.)

That's when I notice Ed and Delia are actually  UGH! HOLDING HANDS.

It's **HORRIBLE.**

I feel a bit sick and have to run into the house quickly.

I grab my guitar, teddy, AND a selection of embarrassing photos of Delia that I've been saving for a VERY special occasion.

I think this might be the SPECIAL occasion I've been waiting for.

Delia with a potty on her head

Delia after cutting her own hair with play scissors

Delia with scary smile

Delia after I pushed her into the mud (my personal favorite)

Delia with more bad hair and zits

Derek can't stop laughing at Delia's OLD photos.

We both agree that photos this funny need to be shared with OTHER people.

Other people like

Delia's boyfriend, ED.

(I have a VERY good plan.)

We cleverly attach all the photos (plus a few extra drawings) to Derek's fishing line. Then we dangle them out of the window just behind Delia's head.

Our plan seems to be working.

Ed is **laughing** a lot. Unlike Delia, who is wondering what he's laughing at.

Luckily, we manage to pull up the photos before Delia works out what's going on. At least they're not holding hands anymore.

SUCCESS!

(It's a good start to the sleepover.)

WARNING
Delia has worms
TRUE
Delia is a FREAK
What's so funny?
Tom is . . .
WOOF! WOOF!

next. Mr. Fingle (Derek's dad) is hovering outside the garage where we practice. Derek says we can't start until his dad is OUT of the way completely.

This is because his dad likes to give us tips on music, which Derek finds very embarrassing. Mind you, my dad is EXACTLY the same. (What is it with dads and music? ♫ ♫ ♪) Mr. Fingle keeps his record collection and record player in the garage.

All his records are in alphabetical order and Derek says he spends HOURS cleaning them and looking at the covers.

(How sad is that?)

Anytime we go to practice, Mr. Fingle will suddenly appear and say things like,

Derek warns me . . .
"If my dad EVER says to you,
'Have you heard of this band, Tom?'
just say
YES.
What happens if I say NO?
I ask.
"You'll be forced to listen to CRACKLY OLD records FOREVER. So trust me. Just say
YES
and pretend you know all about the band already."
OK,
I agree.

He's still there.

We wait until Mr. Fingle is safely out of the way before sneaking in and getting started.

we need to learn a few more songs. Which won't be easy because right now the ONLY song we can play all the way through (just about) is DELIA'S A WEIRDO.

Which goes like this. . . .

Delia's a Weirdo

Who's that weirdo over there?
Dressed in **black**
With greasy hair
You can't trust her
She's not nice
She's got no heart
Just a block of ice

CHORUS

Delia
She's a WEIRDO
Delia
She's a GEEK
Delia
She's a WEIRDO
Delia
She's a FREAK

Delia's a grumpy moo
Don't let her
Stand next to you
Big black glasses
Hide her eyes
She really smells
And that's no lie

CHORUS

Delia enjoying
the song

Derek plays me a song called

(It's an oldie his dad taught him.)

It's ACE! But I think we might need another band member to play it properly.

I don't think Derek can keep playing drums and keyboard . . .

at the same time.

Luckily, Derek agrees.

We are chatting about how to find a new band member when his dad suddenly appears.

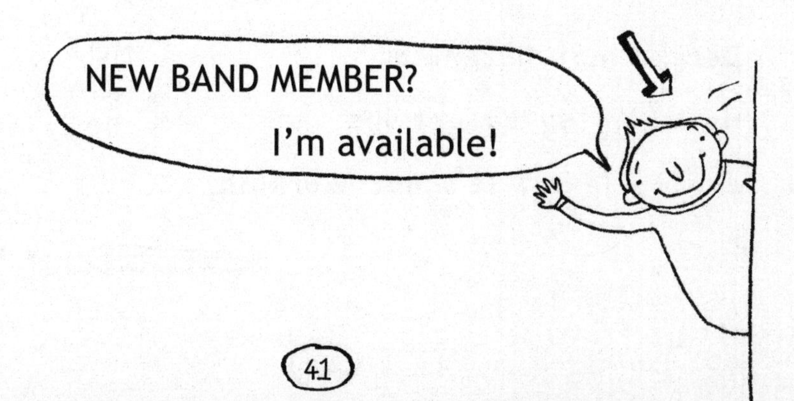

Derek says, "We're busy, Dad," but Mr. Fingle doesn't take the hint.

"What are you playing, lads?"

I say. Derek gives me a "What did you say THAT for?" look.

"'Wild Thing.' Good choice, boys. Didn't I teach you that, Derek?"

Derek's not listening. He is trying to get his dad to leave. It's not working.

"Do you know who played the original version of 'Wild Thing'?" Mr. Fingle asks.

(In my head I'm thinking about what Derek told me.)

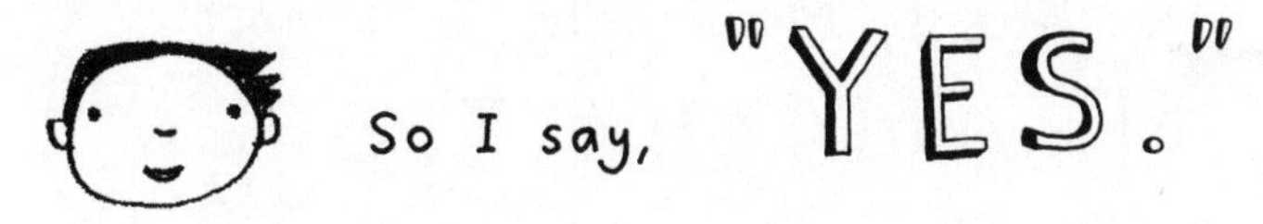

Then Mr. Fingle says,

"Really? Most people remember **the Troggs'** version, but the Wild Ones were first to record it, in 1965."

Now it gets tricky.

Mr. Fingle then asks me,

"Have you heard of **the Troggs**, Tom?"

And for a split second I forget what I'm supposed to say (because I've said YES already, and I don't want to be rude). I hear myself saying,

And that's it. . . . He's Off!

Looking through his record collection to play us both versions of "Wild Thing."

Derek rolls his eyes and says we might as well leave him to it.

"He won't even notice we're gone," Derek says.

He's right.

Derek and I spend the rest of the evening chit-chatting about Delia's dodgy photos (VERY funny).

And how **BRILLIANT** it was sneaking back to my house and sticking even MORE photos around when Delia wasn't looking!

Delia's photos + me and Derek = Genius

Mrs. Worthington's mustache gets a mention, too.

It's getting late and I'm really tired, but I don't want to be the first one to go to sleep because I'm waiting for the right moment to bring out my teddy.

Then Derek says that "JUST FOR TONIGHT" he's going to use his teddy as a PILLOW because it helps him sleep.

And I say, "That's SUCH a good idea!" And take my teddy out, too.

Then we eat some snacks . . .

and a few more. Until we both fall fast asleep zzzzzzzzzzzzzzzzz

So far I'm having a very good holiday and NOT missing school at all. I'm keeping busy by doing all kinds of GOOD STUFF like:

- Finding NEW places to hide Delia's sunglasses.

☺ Sleepovers at Derek's.

☺ Listening to DUDE 3 and trying out new ROCK STAR poses.

☺ More drawing and doodling.

This is a good game:

Do a scribble

then see what you can turn it into.

Like ⇧ this . . . ALIENS!

This game is particularly good to play in BORING lessons, as it looks like you are VERY busy.

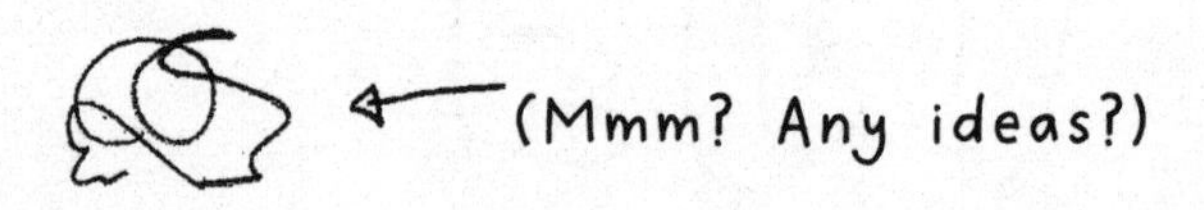

I am perfectly happy and have ☺ **LOADS** of ideas for more drawings when Dad comes in and interrupts.

Are you ready?

"What for?"

"Remember? You're staying at your cousins' for the afternoon."

"What for?"

"Because your mom and I are both working. It's just for a few hours."

"Can I go to Derek's?"

"The Fingles are out shopping today."

"You mean Granny and Granddad?
They're out and about, too."

"I'll stay here with Delia."

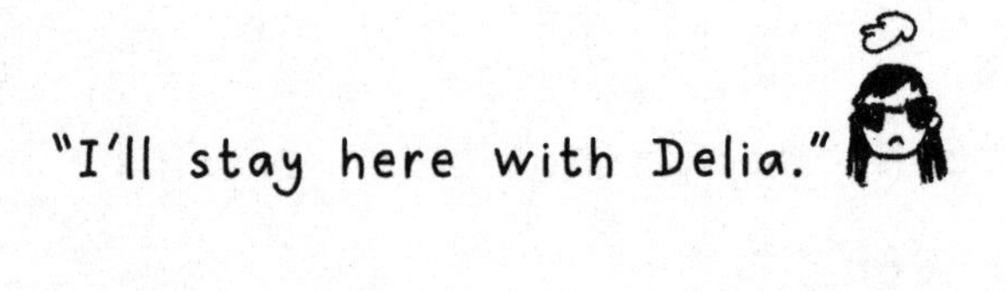

"You must be desperate, Tom. She's going out. Sorry, you have to go to your cousins'. Just try not to do anything silly . . . like last time."

(The Fossils "out and about")

GROAN . . . looks like I don't have much choice. Then Dad adds,

"Oh, and **PLEASE** DO **NOT** mention my birthday to Uncle Kevin or Auntie Alice. I don't want any fuss this year."

"OK."

"And don't mention how many parking tickets I have. Uncle Kevin doesn't need to know."

"OK."

There seem to be a LOT of things I'm not allowed to mention to Uncle Kevin and Auntie Alice. I sometimes don't remember them all.

Last time I was there for a visit, Uncle Kevin kept asking Dad about his job. And I heard Dad say,

"Well, I've just moved to a fantastic NEW office that is much closer to home. So I do a lot less traveling and it's far more suitable for my work." So I said . . .

Which is **TRUE!**

But Dad gave me one of those "What did you have to say that for?" stares.

I definitely don't mention the tin of biscuits he keeps in the shed because I know that's a secret.

Occasionally my cousins play tricks on me. Hee, hee

Some tricks are funnier than others.

This one was annoying.

It was **REALLY** embarrassing when Auntie Alice followed the chocolate footprints right back to me.

(One reason I don't want to go to the cousins'.)

So I am (very slowly) getting ready to go when Delia comes up to me and says,

"If you're going to the cousins', will you do me a favor?"

"What?"

"DON'T COME BACK . . . EVER."

SUDDENLY I think of some **GOOD** reasons to go after all.

1. Delia won't be there to annoy me. ☺

2. They keep **LOTS** of cakes and biscuits in the house.

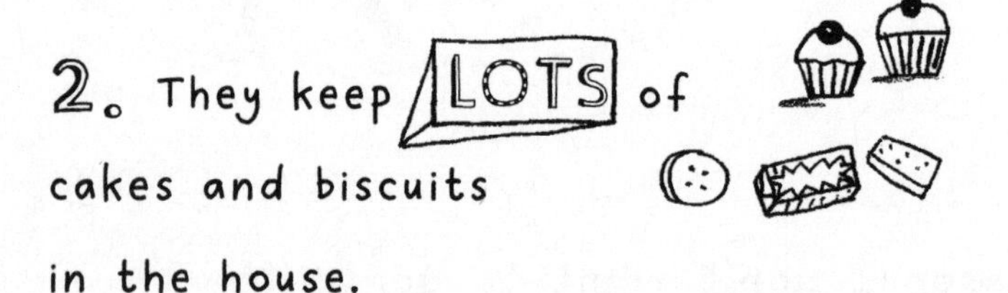

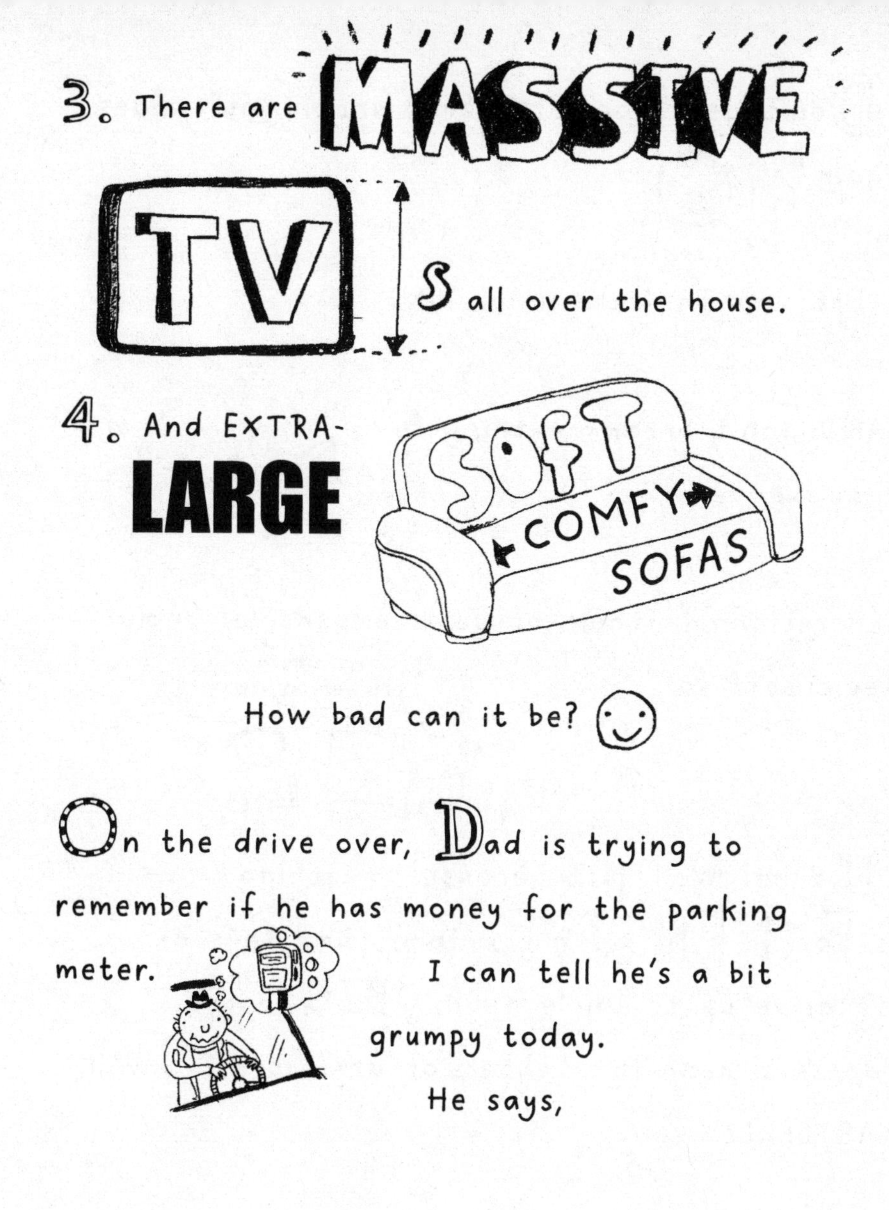

3. There are MASSIVE TVs all over the house.

4. And EXTRA-LARGE SOFT COMFY SOFAS

How bad can it be? 🙂

On the drive over, Dad is trying to remember if he has money for the parking meter. I can tell he's a bit grumpy today.

He says,

"Don't get chocolate stuck under your shoes again."

(That was the cousins' fault!)

"AND don't break anything that's expensive."

"Everything in their house is expensive, Uncle Kevin said so."

"Did he? Well just because something is **EXPENSIVE**, Tom," Dad says as we drive up to Uncle Kevin's **BIG** house, "doesn't mean it's better, or any more . . . well, TASTEFUL."

Dad is very pleased Uncle Kevin has already gone. "I can park in his space for free," he says.

Auntie Alice opens the door and tells us,

"You've just missed your Uncle Kevin!"

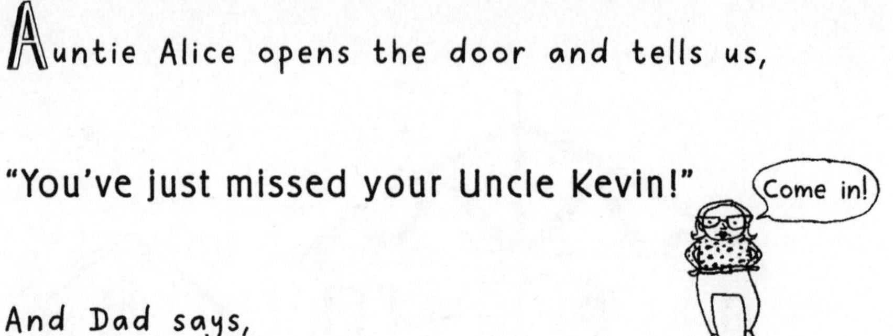

And Dad says,
"What a SHAME! We did try to get here earlier."

(We didn't.)

Then Dad thanks Auntie Alice for having me over and promises not to be too long.

BYE!

I go and find the cousins, who are busy eating snacks

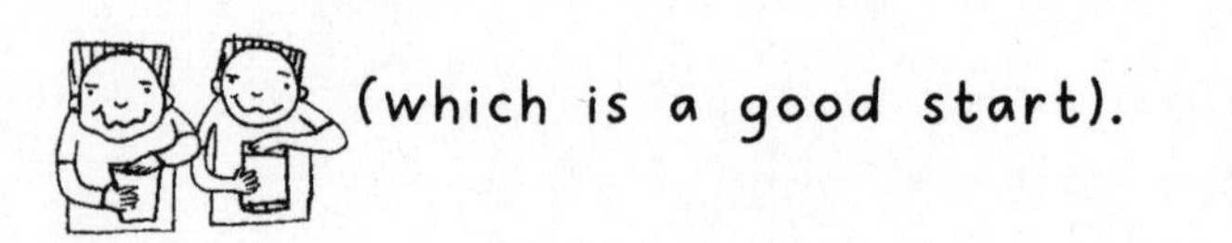

(which is a good start).

But they don't seem keen on sharing their snacks with me.

Instead we go to the food cupboard (which is **STUFFED** full of treats). The cousins tell me to help myself.

"You're a guest, take those biscuits . . . they're nice."

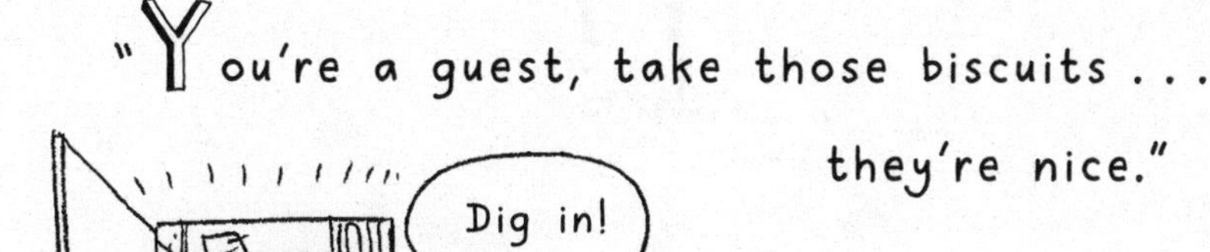

BRILLIANT!

(It would be rude not to.)

I manage to CRAM LOTS into my pockets and carry the rest in a BIG pile.

Which is so high I can't see where I'm going. The cousins help out by shouting directions.

"Forward."

"Forward."

"Keep going. . . .

Keep going . . . KEEP GOING . . .

WHOOPS!"

I walk

BANG

SMACK into Auntie Alice.

Who suggests I

put a few snacks back.

(I think the cousins have tricked me.) I'm allowed to keep the caramel wafers and a drink. Which is good news because at least I get to do the "empty biscuit wrapper" joke on the cousins. . . .

Which they fall for

EVERY TIME.

(It's hilarious.)

When the cousins have had enough of my little biscuit joke, I suggest we watch TV instead.

"GOOD IDEA," they say.

"Let's watch something FUNNY?"

I add. But the cousins want to watch a

SCARY film. (Which is not my idea

of fun at ALL.)

I blame Delia. She let me

watch

THE HOUSE WITH THE DEADLY EYES

when I was little. She thought it was funny

making me JUMP.

(It wasn't.)

Instead I say,

"I'll watch ANYTHING."

They choose . . .

(Mmm, doesn't look too bad?)

OK, I'm wrong.

The film turns out to be <u>the</u> most

film I have EVER seen. I have to hide behind a cushion for most of it. Unlike the cousins, who can't stop LAUGHING! They think it's funny. (It's not.)

I can't wait until it's over.

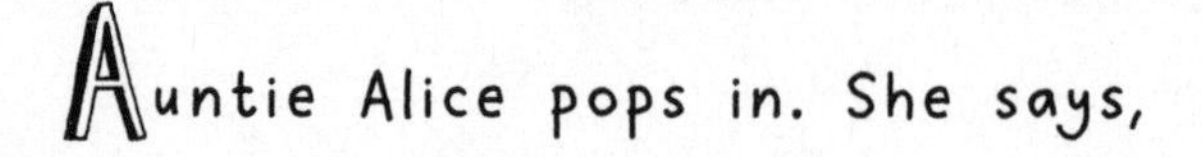

Auntie Alice pops in. She says,

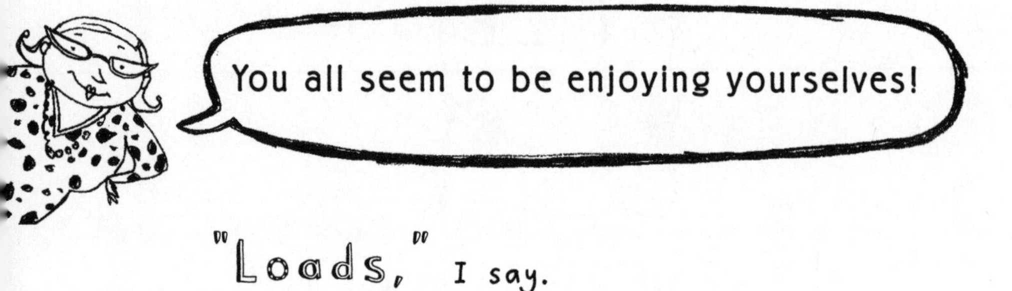

"Loads," I say.

When it's finished, the cousins suggest we watch ANOTHER film. (Groan.)

"A REALLY SCARY film this time."

(What do they mean, a REALLY SCARY one?)

Great, I'll just have to keep my eyes SHUT → ← the ENTIRE time now.

They put on:

So I am hiding behind a cushion again.

It's not helping much.

I can still hear the scary stuff through the cushion.

Luckily Dad turns up early to pick me up.

PHEW!

In front of the cousins, though, I pretend to be VERY sad that I won't get to see the rest of the film. SHAME.

"Maybe next time you're round," the cousins say to me. (I hope not.)

Auntie Alice tells Dad I've been "no trouble at all."

For some reason Dad asks, "No chocolate stains on the carpet or antiques broken, then?"

(Thanks for reminding everyone, Dad.)

"Nothing damaged. But speaking of old antiques, isn't it your birthday soon, Frank?"

And I hear Dad say, "My birthday's not for AGES." Which isn't true at ALL. So I mention that Dad's birthday is actually NEXT WEEK. How could anyone forget their own birthday?

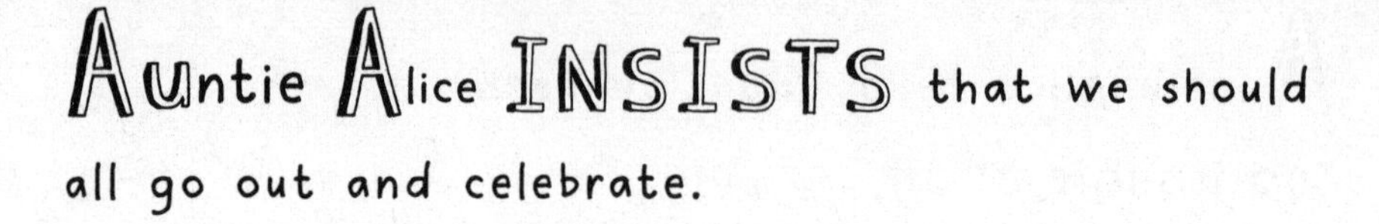
Auntie Alice INSISTS that we should all go out and celebrate.

"Just like last year. It will be

(Dad's birthday present last year)

EXCUSES . . .
EXCUSES . . . ?

Dad doesn't seem keen on the idea. I can tell he's trying very hard to think of reasons not to go when Uncle Kevin bursts in through the door.

“Frank! I hope you paid for parking. There’s a traffic warden looking at your car.”

From the way Dad RUNS out the door, I’m guessing he didn’t pay the meter.

We all follow him outside.

Dad is REALLY CROSS and shouting rude things. Uncle Kevin is shaking his head in a disapproving way.

So I tell Uncle Kevin that HE'D

be CROSS too, if he had TEN

parking tickets like Dad.

Now Dad's cross with ME for saying how many tickets he's got.

Like it's MY FAULT!

Dad's in a REALLY bad mood all the way home. But that's NOTHING compared with how cross MOM is when she finds out that:

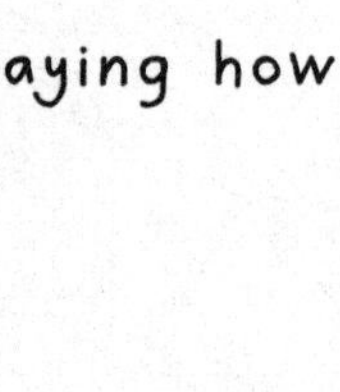

You've done What?

1. Dad got ANOTHER parking ticket  (number eleven).

2. We have to go to dinner with the cousins for Dad's birthday.

3. I watched "VAMPIRE SWAMP MONSTERS FROM HELL." (Well, sort of.)

I don't think I'll be going back to the cousins' again for a while, which means I won't be able to watch the rest of

BLOODSUCKER BEETLES vs. GIANT ALIENS.

(RESULT!)

During the night I wake up with a HORRIBLE PAIN in my Agh! tooth. I sneak to the bathroom to take a proper look.

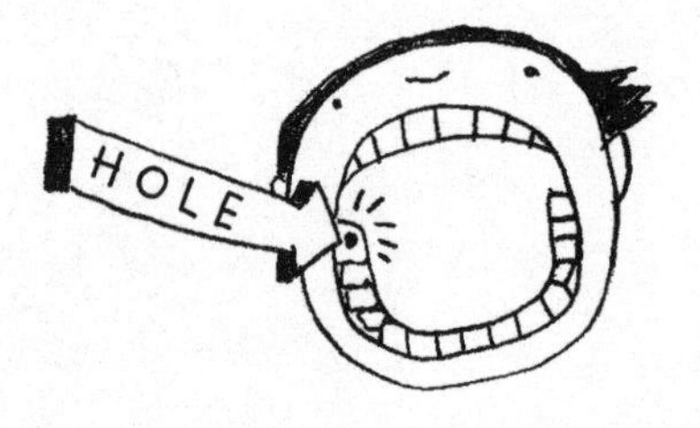

It's not good.
I can see a BIG black hole in it . . .
oh, no. . . .
Groan.

I brush my teeth in the hope that the hole will suddenly close up and go away.

It doesn't.

It just HURTS even more.

Which means I'll probably HAVE to go to the DENTIST now.

GROAN.

If Mom finds out I have a toothache, she won't let me have ANY sweets or snacks for a while. And she DEFINITELY won't let me take treats over to DEREK'S house.

Mom's treats

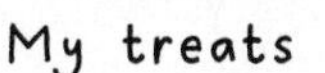

My treats

TOO late.

Mom must have heard me in the bathroom groaning and has woken up.

I'm poking my tooth when she knocks on the door. I tell Mom that I can't sleep because I have a headache. **And** I'm having bad dreams from watching the **SCARY** film at the cousins'.

Poor TOM

Mom gives me some medicine (which brilliantly stops my tooth hurting).

I go back to bed and try to get some sleep.

ZZZZZZZZZZZZZ

But in the morning my toothache is BACK.

And if that's not bad enough . . .

the first thing DELIA says to me is,

GREAT. Mom must have told her I woke up in the night. On top of calling me a scaredy-cat, she keeps on sneaking up behind me and saying

which is getting on my nerves.

So I do this drawing to cheer myself up.

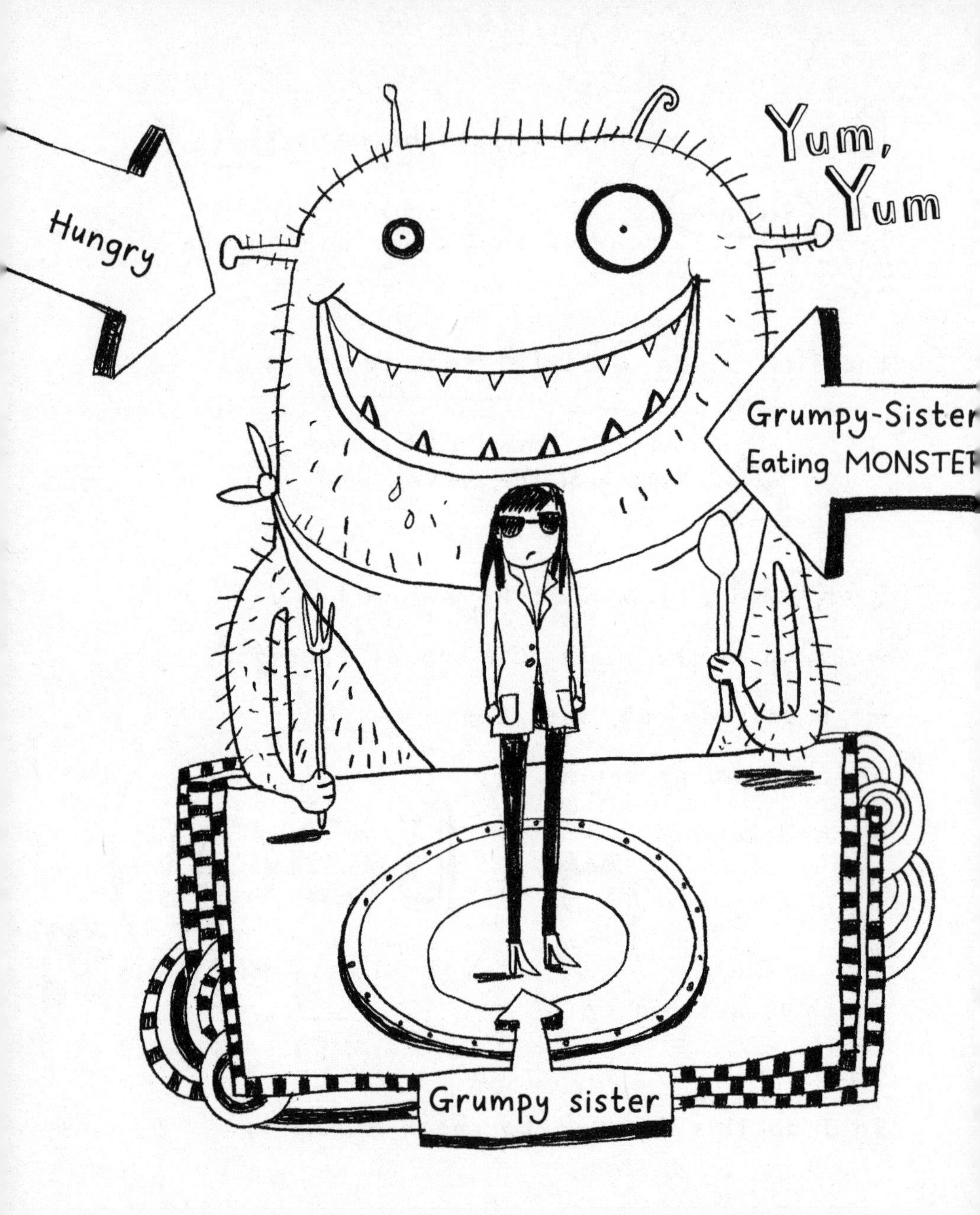
Hungry
Yum, Yum
Grumpy-Sister
Eating MONSTER
Grumpy sister

I'm eating breakfast on the non-painful side of my mouth (and trying not to drool) when Derek comes over and asks if I want to go swimming.

(Which **might** take my mind off this toothache.)

So I say **yes** and hope for the best. At least Delia won't be there to annoy me.

What's more irritating—Delia or a toothache?

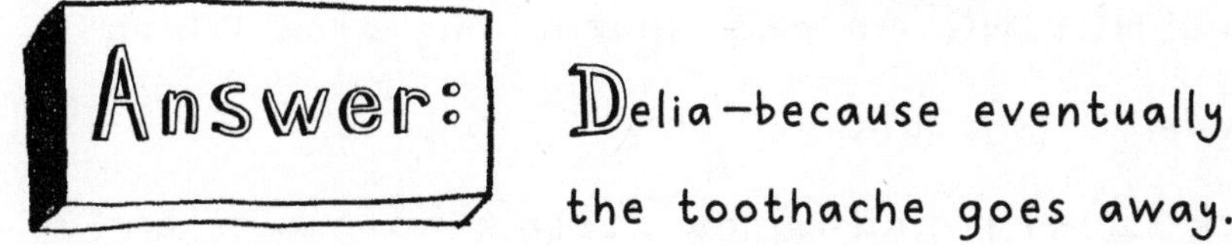

Delia—because eventually the toothache goes away.

I've been groaning

a bit due to my tooth THROBBING, Derek asks me if I'm OK. I don't mention my toothache because I'm hoping the water will SOOTHE my face and make the pain go away completely.

AND Derek has TREATS for after swimming that he said he'd share with me. Instead I tell him that my groaning is due to Delia SHOVING me and injuring my arm. Which is true . . . she did.

Derek is very glad he doesn't have a sister.

When we get to the pool, it's pretty busy already. I spot quite a few kids from our school swimming, including . . .

Amy is the smartest girl in the school, which is excellent for me as I get to take the occasional sneaky peek at her work.

The girls are too busy chatting and swimming and don't see us come in.

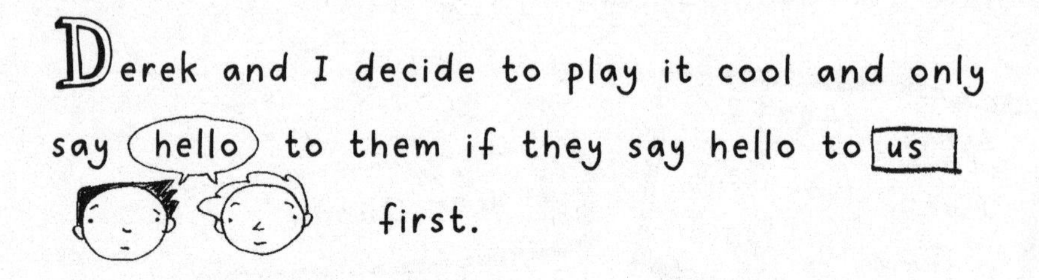

Derek and I decide to play it cool and only say hello to them if they say hello to us first.

(Good plan.)

So we go off to get changed, and I'm

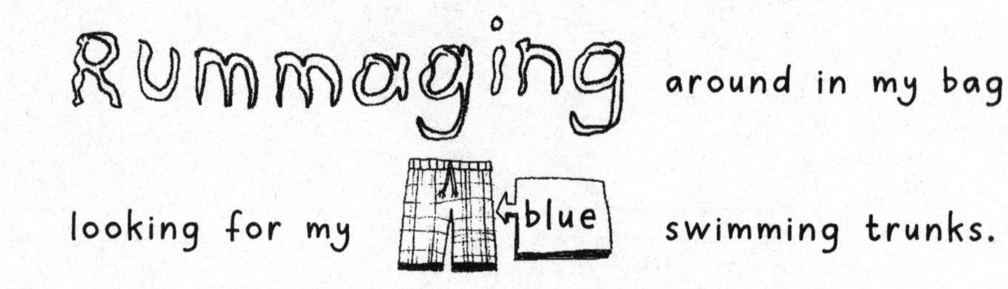

Rummaging around in my bag looking for my blue swimming trunks.

I can't find them ANYWHERE.

I have a HORRIBLE feeling I've left them at home. (I did.)

Derek makes two suggestions:

1. I should swim in my PANTS.
(That's not going to happen.)

2. He has a very OLD pair of trunks in his bag I can borrow.

I say, "GREAT." At least I'll be able to swim now.
Derek passes them to me under the changing-room door.

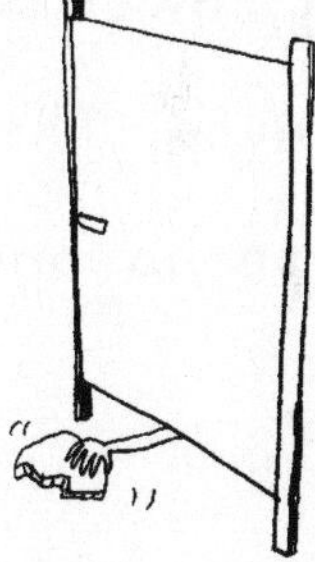

When I see them, I'm wondering exactly how old these trunks really are? The teddy-bear pattern makes me think Derek was probably about FOUR when he last wore them.

They are a bit short so I have to keep my towel round me until the very LAST minute. Then I quickly jump in the pool and hope no one has seen me.

Derek and I swim up and down and dive to the bottom, which is fun. ☺

(It makes me forget about my toothache. Well, almost.)

Amy and her friends still haven't seen us yet, but **Norman Watson** has.

He's waving like **CRAZY** from the other side of the pool. Norman's brought his little brother with him, who looks just like him only smaller. They come and join us, which is good because now we can all play **SHARK** together.

Derek is the SHARK first.
He manages to swim and catch me. Now it's
my turn to be the SHARK.
YEAH!
I spot
Norman (who's not great at hiding) and quickly
swim to catch him. Now Norman is the
SHARK. I've never seen Norman swim
before, so it's a bit of a surprise when he
starts to
SPLASH!
He's not moving much, just . . .

SPLASHING!
AND
SPLASHING!
AND
SPLASHING!

His arms and legs are thrashing around making MASSIVE waves in the pool. The splash is SO huge the lifeguard looks over and blows her whistle.

We're all told to:

The lifeguard dives in and "rescues" Norman (who's **not** drowning, just swimming VERY badly).

Everybody is standing at the side of the pool watching (including Amy, Florence, and Indrani).

While Norman is explaining to the lifeguard about his "unusual swimming style," the lifeguard tells us,

"No more *crazy* splashing or you'll have to LEAVE!"

It's VERY embarrassing.

Then if THAT'S not bad enough, Amy comes over and says to me,

"Nice teddy swimming trunks, Tom."

(I'd forgotten all about my teddy-bear swimming trunks . . . groan.)

And I can hear Florence and Indrani laughing.

I jump back in the pool quickly to hide.

Norman's little brother, Alfie, jumps in, too, and wants to challenge me to a race.

He's only small; I don't want to hurt his feelings . . .

so I give him a head start.

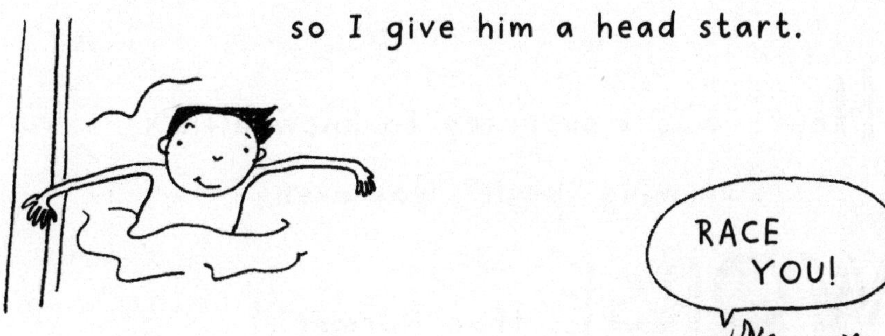

How was I supposed to know Alfie's swimming "style" was even **WORSE** than Norman's?

(The lifeguard has seen enough splashing for one day.)

It was a short swim, but on the way home I realize that my toothache has completely g o n e.

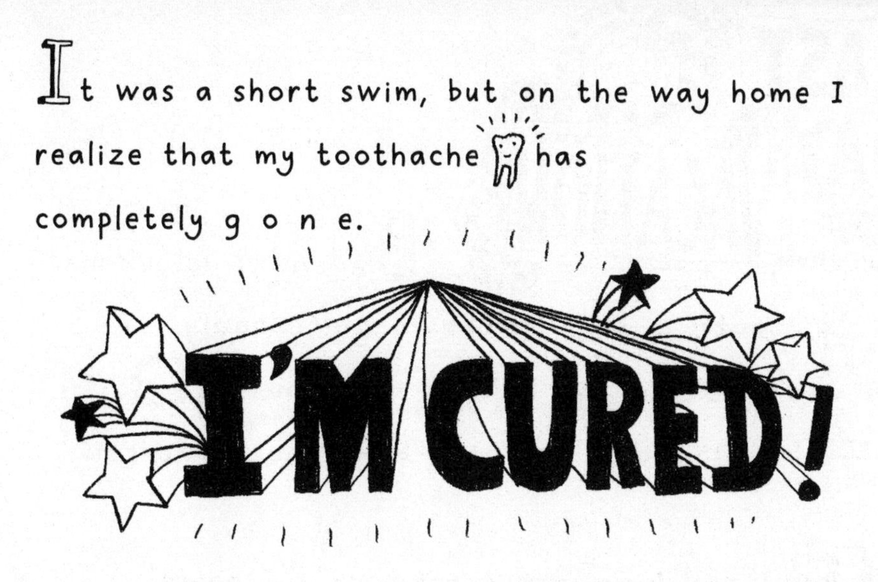

I won't have to go to the dentist after all now.

BRILLIANT!

I celebrate by taking the very small sweet that Derek offers me.

(Which is a mistake.)

LAST DAY OF VACATION

Bad news is . . . my tooth is still throbbing quite badly.

I can't believe the holiday has gone SO *FAST* and I'm back at school tomorrow.

If I tell Mom about my tooth, I could probably get the day off school. But that would mean having to:

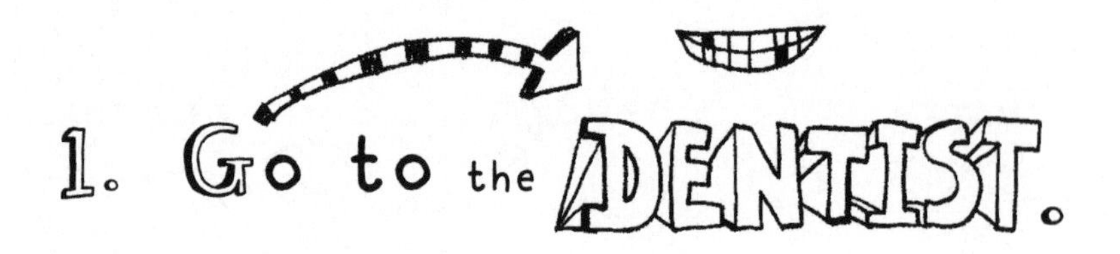

2. Get stuff done to my tooth.

3. Not eat TREATS or any sweet stuff for a very long time.

4. Catch up on the schoolwork I missed.

Instead I try to forget all about my toothache by doing some drawing.

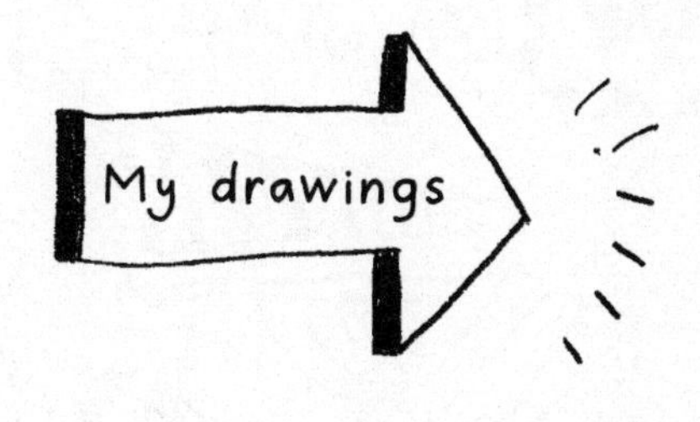

Toothbrush Monster
help!
SMILE!
AGH!

I'm **STILL** thinking about my **TOOTHACHE.**

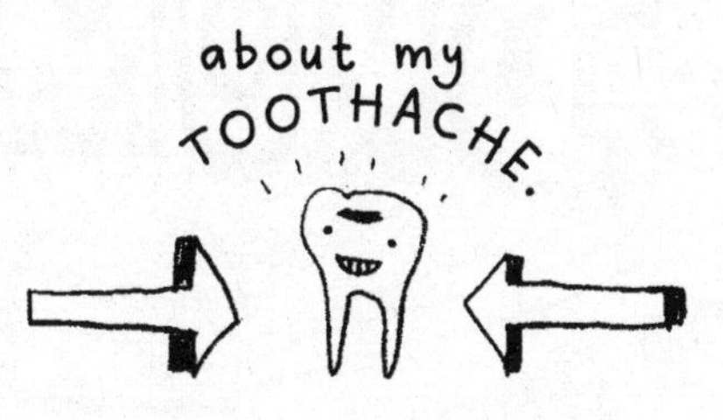

(Groan.)

I know, I'll do a **BIG** poster for **DOGZOMBIES** instead.

Derek and I definitely want a drummer for the band. We can put the poster on the school notice board tomorrow.

It will GRAB everyone's attention.

(That's the plan, anyway.)

WANTED
DRUMMER
FOR BRILLIANT NEW BAND
DOGZOMBIES
MUST LIKE DUDE3
be able to DRUM (a bit)
AUDITIONS
AT DEREK'S HOUSE IN HIS GARAGE WITH
TOM GATES AND DEREK FINGLE
WRITE YOUR NAME HERE
(Unless you are an ANNOYING person)
(We like nice biscuits if you want to bring some.)

That should do the trick.

(Tooth still hurting, though.)

I'm struggling to get out of bed even more than usual. (I didn't sleep so well; tooth still throbbing.) School starts in half an hour and I have a LOT of things to remember today, like . . .

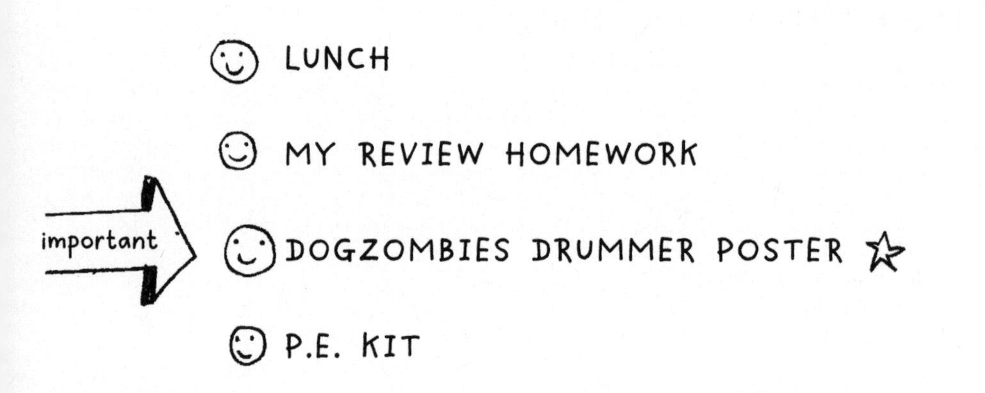

(Or I'll be forced to wear something from the SPARE KIT BOX.)

NO
SPARE KIT BOX

I eat breakfast carefully (on the good side of my mouth). Mom tells me to

She thinks I'm suffering from "BacktoSchoolitis."

"Very common on the first day back at school."

Delia says, "He's got

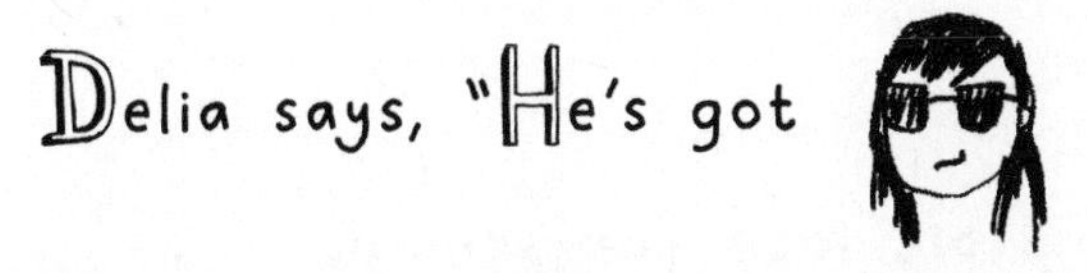

IRRITATING BROTHER SYNDROME."

(She's SO annoying.)

Dad asks me, "Have you got your lunch? Got your homework?"

"Got worms?" Delia adds.

Normally I would defend myself with

a HILARIOUS and funny answer. But I think the toothache has stopped that part of my brain from working properly . . .

for now.

Derek and I are a bit late for school. We try to do fast walking while I show Derek the

He's impressed and offers to put the poster up for me.

"You'll forget," he says.

(Harsh but true.)

Back in class, it's like we've never been away. Marcus Meldrew manages to ANNOY me within TWO seconds of sitting down at my desk.

He pulls up his school sweater and shows me his T-shirt.

I can't believe it!

He's wearing a special DUDE3 T-shirt that the WHOLE band has signed!

"It's NEW and my mom's hand-stitched over the band's REAL signatures so they won't EVER wash out."

"I'm ffwwilled for you, Marcus," I say.

(My tooth is throbbing, so I'm finding it hard to speak properly.)

Mr. Fullerman begins to take attendance and I answer,

"Earrrrr, suuurrrrr."

He thinks I'm trying to be funny.

Ha! Ha! (I'm not!)

Then the class starts laughing and Mr. Fullerman peers over the register.

His beady eyes are fixed on ME.

He says,

"TOM . . . I hope you've remembered your REVIEW HOMEWORK. You've had two weeks to do it. And a letter to remind you."

And I say, "Eeeerrrrrrrrrr" (to give myself time to think).

Because I CAN'T believe I've forgotten it!

What I SHOULD have said to Mr. Fullerman is:

"Sorry, sir. I have done it, but I forgot it. I'll bring it in tomorrow."

I apologize.

But for some STUPID reason I hear myself saying:

"Sir, it's like this. . . .
My dad got a really BAD LURGY bug over the holidays, then we ALL got it. The doctor said it was VERY catching and the germs could be EVERYWHERE, including the paper I wrote my homework on.

So I just have to write it out again on LURGY-FREE paper just to be on the safe side.

HOMEWORK REVIEW CLOSE-UP

I'll bring it in tomorrow . . .

promise."

(Why, why? Why did I say that?)

Mr. Fullerman says,

"Tom, is there something wrong with your mouth?"

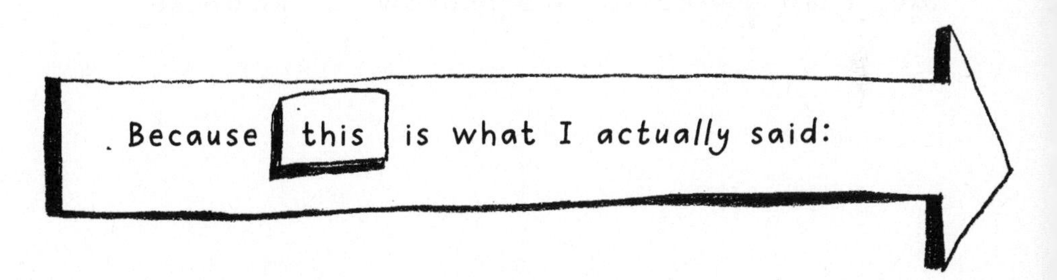

"Errr, it's wike thisss. . . .

My daaa go a wearrrly add WURGY bug ower the howidays, hen we AWW go it. The doctow said it was verwy caaching and thw erms coowld bee EVERRWYWHERE, incwuding th aper I wwott eye omeworwk on.

Seww I ust ave too wwitte it owwt again on WURRGY-FWWEE apper usst to ee on the affe ide. I'ww bwing it in ommorow . . . pwomise."

I managed to mutter,

"Sore twooth, sirr. . . . I'm OK, wrreally."

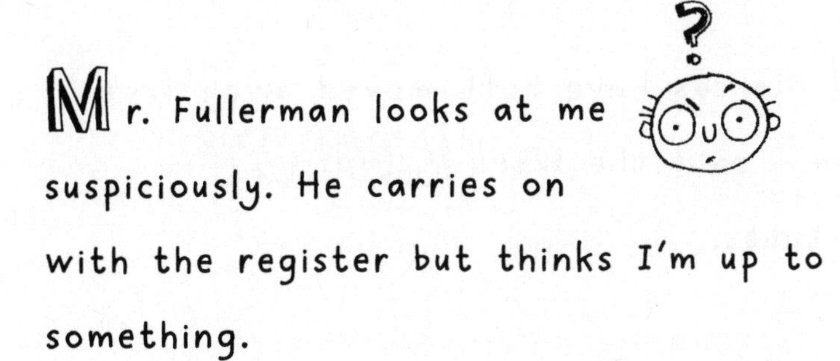

Mr. Fullerman looks at me suspiciously. He carries on with the register but thinks I'm up to something.

(Like I'm doing this deliberately!)

Amy and Marcus have both moved away from me because I said the word **LURGY** too many times.

"I have twoothache . . . not the LURGY," I tell Amy.

(She **might** feel sorry for me.)

But she's ignoring me and staring at the classroom door.

"Tom, isn't that your dad waving at you?"

My dad? ⊙⊙

I look up and see someone who looks a bit like my dad?

IT IS MY DAD.

He's trying to get my attention by waving my homework around. (It looks like he's swatting flies.) Groan.

Now EVERYONE is STARING at him, including Mr. Fullerman, who goes over to the door. He looks a bit CROSS at being disturbed.

Dad starts talking to him . . . ha! ha! and they BOTH start LAUGHING.

ha! ha!

What's SO funny?

(This is going to be embarrassing, I can feel it.)

Mr. Fullerman takes my work and Dad makes a thumbs-up sign at me

(with the whole class still watching).

Then Mr. Fullerman comes in and says in front of EVERYONE:

"Tom, your dad has very kindly dropped in your review homework. He also assures me that he's totally LURGY-free and so is your homework. Which must be a HUGE relief to the WHOLE CLASS, I'm sure."

(The shame. . . .)

At least Mr. Fullerman has my homework now . . . I suppose.

I hope today gets better.

(Though it's not looking promising.)

It's no good.

My tooth is hurting SO much.

I can't concentrate anymore groan.

Mr. Fullerman sees that my face has

SWELLED UP

a LOT. He sends me straight to the nurse's office.

On the way to the nurse's office, I walk past some little kids who stare at me like I'm some kind of MONSTER.

Even Mrs. Mumble in the school office looks concerned. She rings my dad straightaway. He's just gotten home when he has to head right back to school.

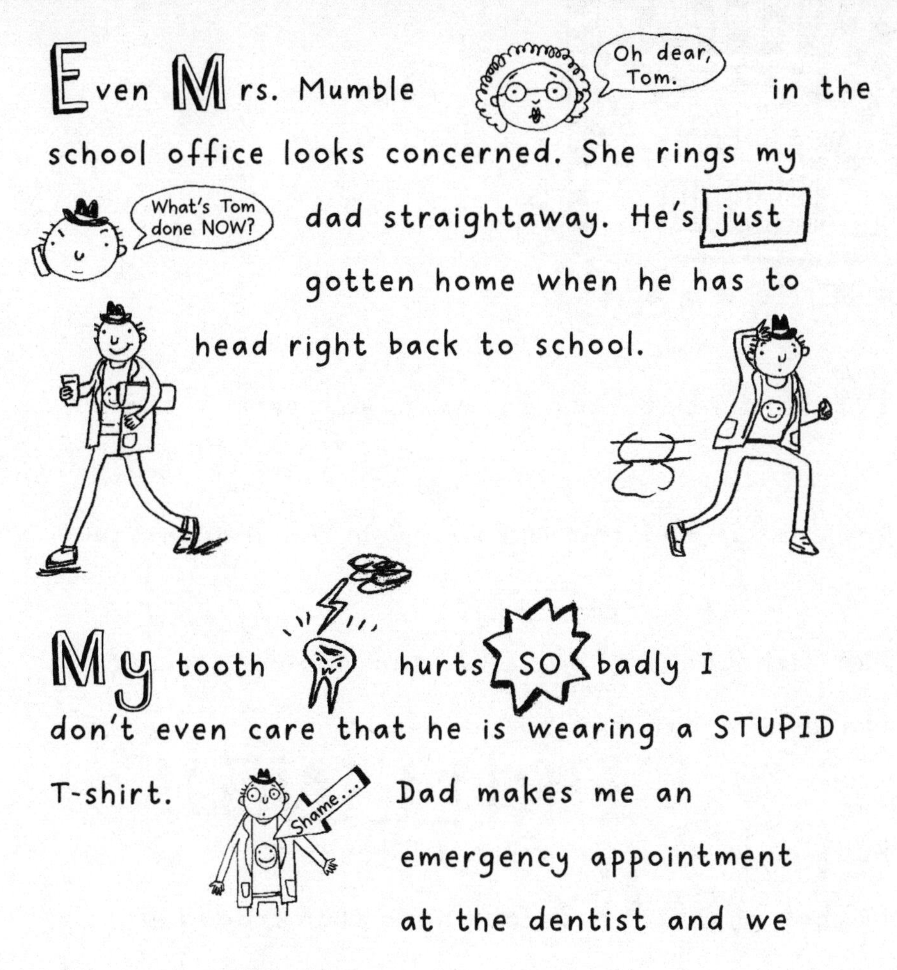

My tooth hurts SO badly I don't even care that he is wearing a STUPID T-shirt. Dad makes me an emergency appointment at the dentist and we drive straight there.

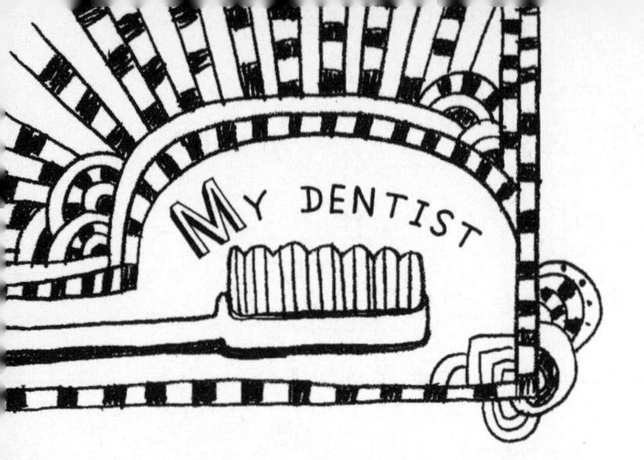

Most dentists try to make you feel

chilled and relaxed by having things

like fish tanks 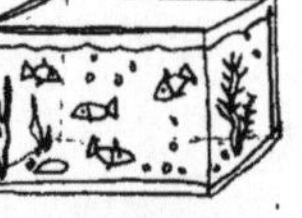 and soothing music

(to drown out the sound of

DRILLING).

But my dentist is a bit different.

He has a SCARY-looking metal crocodile

with sharp teeth on the wall. As well as

posters of people with rotten

teeth and gum diseases.

(I think he's trying to make a point.)

GUM DISEASE
BRUSH THEM OR LOSE THEM
SAVE YOUR TEETH
DECAY
TERRIBLE Teeth
ROTTEN

Dr. Kay takes a look at me and says,

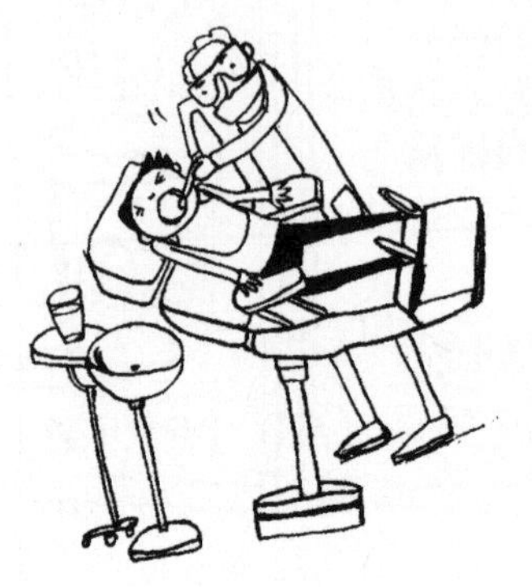

"Mmmmm, not good, young man."

(Like I don't know that already.) Then he picks at my tooth with one of those horrid metal pokey things.

"ARGH!!" I scream, and he says,

"Does that hurt?"

(Errrrr, YES! LOTS!)

Apparently when I was little I once BIT a dentist.

Now Mom thinks that they have a

warning on my file like this:

Dr. Kay explains EVERYTHING to me before he does it. (In case I turn vicious.)

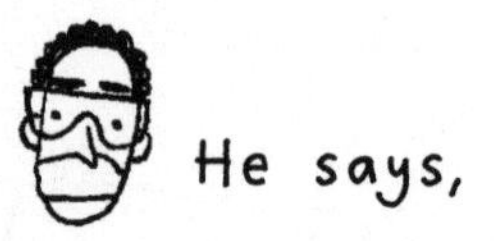

He says,

"Raise your hand if you feel any pain at all."

So I raise my hand . . . even though he hasn't started yet.

Groan . . . now he has.

I get through the injections, drilling, and filling by keeping my eyes tightly shut and thinking of different ways to get back at Delia for teasing me.

When I do open them, I can see a **WEIRD** mobile hanging from the ceiling.

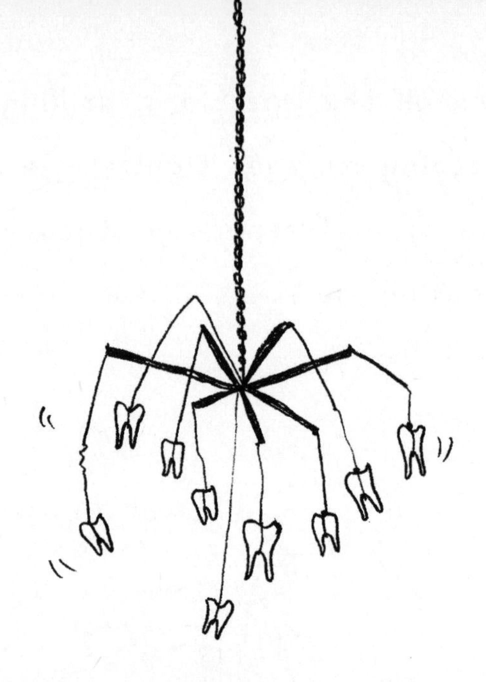

I think it's made of teeth?

It is made of teeth.

Dr. Kay points at it and says, **"That's what happens when you don't look after your teeth."**

It's really freaky.

I'm SO relieved when it's all over. ☺

My face is numb and I end up dribbling the pink water Dr. Kay gives me to swish round my mouth everywhere.

Dad says I am VERY brave.

I agree ☺ and suggest maybe

a small treat might be in order?

Dr. Kay suddenly remembers to give me some

"special stickers."

(They're not exactly my idea of a treat, but I'm guessing something SWEET will be out of the question now?)

Interesting selection of stickers

We stop off to pick up the tablets I have to take (I don't want my face to SWELL up again).

Dad likes my stickers. He thinks it's HILARIOUS that my dentist is called **Dr. D. Kay.**

"A dentist called Dr. D. KAY—that's IRONIC," he says.

I have no idea what he's talking about.

Dad buys me a comic for a treat instead. When we get home, Mom is being very nice to me, too. Unlike Delia,

who thinks it's funny to offer me **SWEETS**.

Then she takes them away, saying, "Oh, sorry, I forgot you've just been to the dentist. Ha! Ha!"

Mom catches Delia tormenting me and tells her off. (Yes, Delia, back off.)

Then Mom says that I can eat my (non-chewy) dinner on a tray in front of the telly without Delia bothering me.

It's bliss.

After dinner Dad reminds me to take my tablet. I'm looking at the bottle and FINALLY I get Dad's dentist name joke . . .

Dr. D. Kay.

Dr. Decay.

Hilarious!

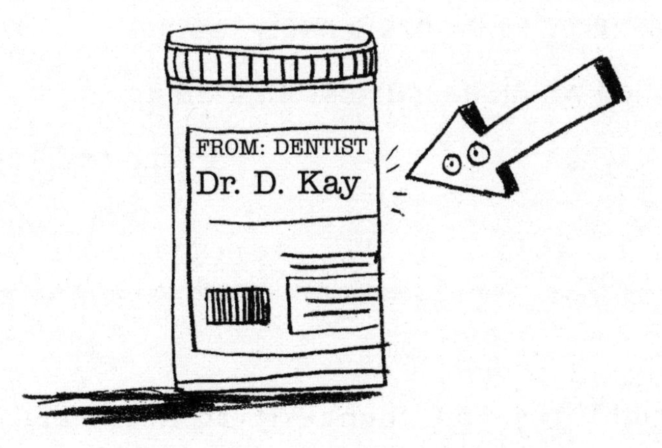

This morning Mom says I am well enough to go to school today despite me doing a "sad face." (It was worth a try.)

At least she gives me a REAL sick note that says:

Dear Mr. Fullerman,

Please could Tom be excused from P.E. just for now as he has a nasty tooth infection which has almost cleared up.

Kind regards,

Rita Gates

But I might try and change it to ALL WEEK or ALL MONTH.

(Give it a go?)

At school, I'm busy telling a group of friends about my **DEADLY** and **DANGEROUS** tooth experience.

"It took my dentist ~~one~~ ~~two~~ ~~three~~ SEVEN WHOLE hours to save it AND the dental nurse almost *FAINTED*."

Everyone looks impressed.

So I add, "The dentist said I was very, very brave."

(That bit's true.)

Norman tells us about the time he got his head ⇨ trapped ⇦ in some railings and had to be rescued by firemen. (Why am I not surprised?)

My mate SOLID shows us the scar on his arm from when he fell off his bike.

It looks like a long zipper.

Derek once got stuck in a cat flap.
(He's NEVER told
me that before!)

Then Mark Clump rolls up his trousers and shows us something that looks like two dots on his leg.

"What's that?" I ask.

"Snake bite," he says. We all take a closer look.

Marcus Meldrew pretends he's not very impressed at all.

He says,

"Huh! That's nothing. I was bitten by my new pet."

"Really? Have you got a snake, too, Marcus?" Derek asks.

"My pet is **FAR** more scary than a snake."

"What is it, a man-eating

SPIDER?" I say.

"I've got a VERY BIG new dog.

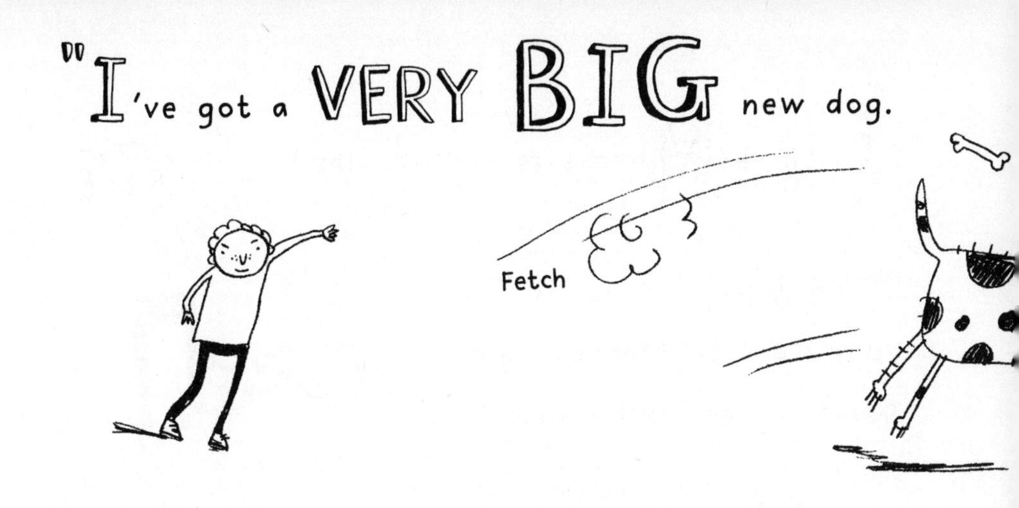

I'm training him right now."

"A dog . . . like how big a dog?"

"HUGE. He's a bit WILD. I had to fight him off and that's when he chewed me. . . . I've got a bad scar."

"Let's see the scar, then?" Norman asks.

"No, it's still VERY painful."

Marcus rubs his leg and walks away with a slight limp.

FAKE limp

(I think Marcus is telling fibs.)

"Mind you," I say, "if I was a dog, I'd bite Marcus, too." Derek agrees with me.

Then Mr. Keen (the headmaster) blows the whistle to go into school and makes us JUMP.

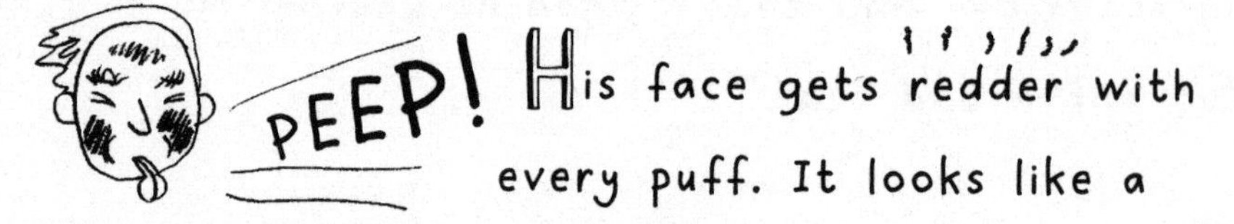

His face gets redder with every puff. It looks like a BIG RED tomato now.

And **that's** when I suddenly remember . . .

This is because last term Mr. Keen heard me singing "Delia's a Weirdo," a song I wrote about Delia.*

He immediately put me in the school concert! Which could have been **total humiliation** in front of the whole school. (Mostly due to lack of practice and slightly rude lyrics about Delia.) Luckily Derek came to my rescue and saved me from possible singing shame.

(* See *The Brilliant World of Tom Gates*, pp. 220–223.)

Mr. Keen thinks I'm upset at missing the school concert.

(I'm **not**.)

I hold my bag up to my face and try to sneak past him. Despite me using small children for extra cover, he sees me.

(Keep walking, keep walking . . .)

"TOM GATES! Just the person I was looking for!"

(Too late.)

"Yes, Mr. Keen."

"I see you're in a BAND with Derek Fingle?"

(How did he know that?)

"And you're looking for a NEW drummer?"

For a TERRIBLE moment I think Mr. Keen wants to join our band until he says,

"Very good poster, by the way."

Phew.

(Derek must have put the poster up yesterday.)

"I know how disappointed you were to miss out on performing in the school concert."

"No, no . . ."

He ignores me.

Mr. Keen then tells me that Mr. Sprocket

(our music teacher) has put together a

SPECIAL

that will be performing in a very important assembly. And GUESS WHAT? Thanks to Mr. Keen, Derek and I are IN the school band NOW.

"Isn't that exciting, Tom?"

I'm lost for words.

"What instrument does Derek play, Tom?"

"Keyboard, Mr. Keen . . . but I don't think—"

Too late—Mr. Keen has already gone.

Oh, no.

Derek won't be happy.

I don't even know what kind of music the school band plays.

I suppose it might be OK? (Extra band practice for DOGZOMBIES at least.)

But Mr. Keen has reminded me about the BAND AUDITION POSTER.

I can't wait to find out WHO wants to be in our band!

On the way to class I go and take a quick look at the poster.

Mmmmmmmmmmmmm.

WANTED
DRUMMER
FOR BRILLIANT NEW BAND
DOGZOMBIES
MUST LIKE DUDE3
be able to DRUM (a bit)
AUDITIONS
AT DEREK'S HOUSE IN HIS GARAGE WITH
TOM GATES AND DEREK FINGLE
WRITE YOUR NAME HERE
(Unless you are an ANNOYING person)
(We like nice biscuits if you want to bring some.)
Mickey Mouse
Norman Watson
Amy Porter
Florence Mitchell
Superman
A Slug
A Worm
Donald Duck

(Oh . . .)

I'm not sure everyone is taking this very seriously.

has added her name!

That's a surprise.

Amy is obviously taking DOGZOMBIES very seriously. Because she is super smart with excellent taste in music. I'll tell Derek the news like this:

"**YEAH! GOOD NEWS!** ☺

Amy Porter is auditioning for the band.

BOO! BAD NEWS. ☹

Mr. Keen has put US in the SCHOOL BAND."

(I'll say the bad news bit really fast. . . . He might not notice.)

In class, Mr. Fullerman asks about my tooth.

How's your tooth, Tom?

So I hand over my

REAL

sick note.

Dear Mr. Fullerman,

Please could Tom be excused from P.E.

the week VERY SERIOUS

just for [illegible] as he has a nasty tooth

infection which has almost cleared up.

Kind regards,

Rita Gates

Mr. Fullerman reads it carefully.

(I hope he doesn't spot my "changes.")

SO far so good.

Then he gives me a LONG ⟶ list of work to catch up on.

I tell Mr. Fullerman this MUST be a mistake because I was only away for one day. Amy says, "You missed loads."

Great.

Now I'm wondering if this is a good time ☺ to mention the DOGZOMBIES audition poster that Amy signed up for. I could give her a few tips?

(Like "Bring caramel wafers.")

But Mr. Fullerman interrupts. He tells us about the **"really exciting school field trip I have planned."**

(Sounds like fun.)

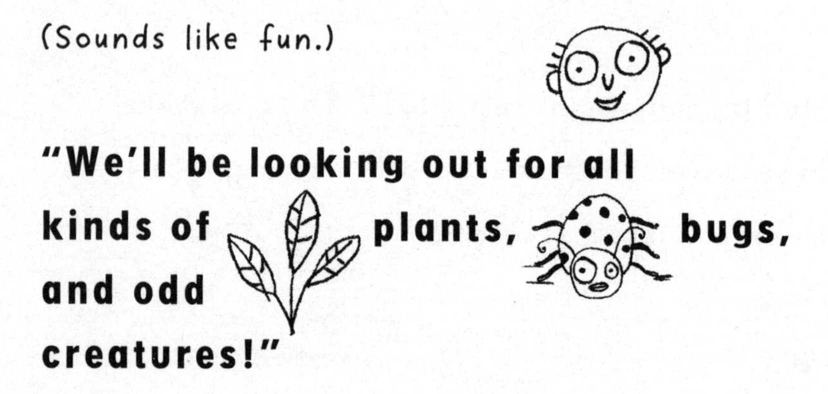

"We'll be looking out for all kinds of plants, bugs, and odd creatures!"

I nudge Amy and point to Marcus. . . .

"Found one."

Forgetting that Mr. Fullerman has

He gives me a teacher stare and says,

"TOM, along with finding odd creatures, I'll be expecting YOU to tell us LOTS of interesting information about trees, as it seems you're a bit of an expert."

Which shuts me up.

I have NO idea why Mr. Fullerman thinks I'm an expert on trees.

A BISCUIT TREE

THIS would be my idea of an INTERESTING TREE.

Next Mr. Fullerman hands out more homework. . . . Groan.

Class 5F Homework
From: Mr. Fullerman
Oakfield School

Dear Class 5F,

This week I want you to write a proper thank-you letter.
You need to decide who you're writing to and what you are thanking them for.
Was it a present or perhaps some good advice?
Use your imagination.
Describe how you feel and remember to lay out the letter correctly.
Looking forward to reading your letters.
Kind regards,

Mr. Fullerman

The homework could be worse, I suppose. At least it's **not** fractions or anything really tricky like that.

How hard is it to say

THANK YOU?

Unless it's to Delia.

But that **NEVER** happens.

When the school day ends, Derek and I are busy discussing Who has signed our DOGZOMBIES audition poster.
So far it's only Amy,
Florence,
and
NORMAN.
I'm guessing SUPERMAN
and MICKEY MOUSE
won't turn up.

I remember to tell Derek that Mr. Keen might want to talk to him about being in the school band.

"I'll just say NO thanks, Sir."

"TOO Late. . . . We're in the school band."

"At least he doesn't know I play keyboard," Derek says.

"He might now.

(It just slipped out, sorry.)"

Derek is wondering what exactly Mr. Keen is planning, when Marcus runs past

REALLY f a s t.

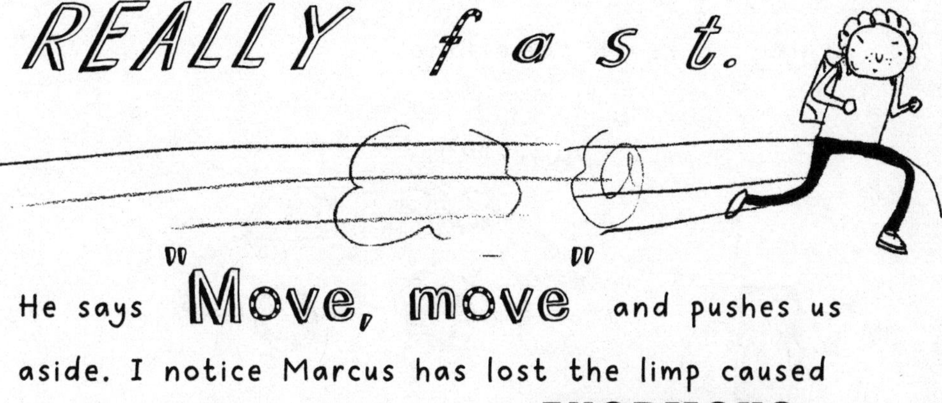

He says "Move, move" and pushes us aside. I notice Marcus has lost the limp caused by the terrible SCAR from his **ENORMOUS** new dog.

"What's the hurry?" I say, but he's already gone.

Derek says, "Let's follow him outside and see what he's up to."

"OK."

Marcus has rushed over to his dad, who's in the car waiting. We watch Marcus open the door and l e a n inside, like he's trying to reach something.

Derek says, "I can hear BARKING!"

"So can I."

"It must be his new dog!"

"The one that BIT him!" I say.

Grrr

We can't see the dog yet but his BARK is VERY LOUD.

Marcus is holding a dog leash and being pulled around.

"Maybe Marcus has a FIERCE dog after all?" Derek says.

"From the way he's struggling to control it, his dog must be really BIG

and STRONG," I say. . . .

Or maybe not.

HOMEWORK

Ever since Mr. Fullerman sent that letter home about my REVIEW HOMEWORK, Mom is being tough on me.

But it's difficult to concentrate because I keep thinking about:

1. Marcus being dragged along by his teeny-weeny dog. **Hilarious!**

2. Dinner.
3. Dinner.
4. The DOGZOMBIES drummer auditions.

It's excellent news that Amy Porter has put her name down. She's so SUPER SMART at EVERYTHING. I can't wait to see how good she is at drumming.

I think this

could work.

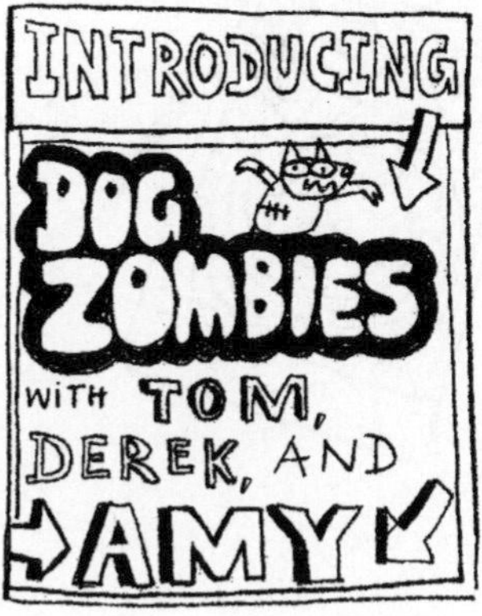

We are holding the auditions
in Derek's garage at the weekend.
Derek's dad, Mr. Fingle, has been BANNED.

Everyone who turns up will have a chance to audition, even if they're rubbish.

As well as the audition, I'm ALSO thinking about . . .

5. Dad's birthday, which is <u>really</u> soon. What to get him?

• Draw a picture?

• Chocolates?

• Socks?

• New hat?

Mom told Auntie Alice

that she had already arranged a little get-together

for Dad to avoid having a party

like last year.

Now EVERYONE is coming over to our house.

Including Granny and Granddad Gates,

or THE FOSSILS as I like to call them,

because they are very

old and ancient.

Which has just given me a GREAT idea

for my THANK-YOU letter homework. Genius . . .

thanks, Fossils.

TO: GRANNY GATES

Dear Granny,

THANK

YOU

FOR THE

POCKET

MONEY.

Love, Tom

(YOUR FAVORITE GRANDSON) x x

Tom,

I have no doubt you are a wonderful grandson.

But I need to see a much longer thank-you letter next time, please.

1 merit.

But well done for joining the NEW SCHOOL BAND. Mr. Keen was extremely pleased.

Mr. Fullerman

Great, now it's **Official.**

Written in black and white by Mr. Fullerman that I **AM** in the school band.

I'm guessing he wasn't impressed with my letter.

And I only got one merit. Which is a bit **harsh,** I think?

Maybe this might help.

To: Mr. Fullerman

Let me explain about the slightly small thank-you letter.

My granny is VERY OLD with dodgy eyes and she falls asleep a lot.

So a thank-you letter needs to be in REALLY BIG WRITING and VERY, VERY SHORT. Or she can't read it. (I am a thoughtful grandson . . . it's true.)

From: Tom Gates

(Hard-working pupil who deserves a few more merits, maybe?)

Space left for EXTRA
merits . . . is still empty.
Oh well, worth a try.

Over the next few days Mr. Fullerman reminds everyone in class that

"REALLY hard-working pupils get the extra merits."

(OK, point taken.)

So I'm doing some EXTRA reading at home when Granny and Granddad pop in for a cup of tea.

I can hear them chit-chatting

Chit

Chat

downstairs with Dad.

I go to say hello (and sneak a biscuit).

Tea + Fossils = BISCUITS

But Dad spots me and says, "No biscuits for you until your tooth infection has cleared up."

Just then Delia comes in and hears the word "INFECTION."

"Ugh . . . disgusting. What's he got now?"

Delia is leaning away from me like I have THE LURGY while helping herself to a biscuit. Right in front of me, too!

"That's not FAIR," I say.

"Delia hasn't got a bad tooth like you," Dad says.

"Ugh, he's Rotting," she laughs, holding her nose.

Granddad says that I **MUST** take care of my teeth or I'll end up looking like him.

Then he says, "Do you want to see what happens to you if you DON'T look after your teeth?"

Granny tries to stop him.

"Don't show him, **Bob**. . . . It's not nice."

NOW I'm *REALLY* curious.

"Your teeth look fine to me, Granddad."

That's when he turns his back . . .

and takes his teeth **OUT** of his mouth!

It's HILARIOUS!

He's got them IN HIS HAND. (OK, that looks weird.)

"See . . . no teeeffff leffft."

Granddad's mouth reminds me of a very old turtle.

Delia says, "That's rank."

Granny tells Granddad to put them back and "don't be so childish."

Which doesn't stop Granddad from pretending to BITE Granny before slipping his teeth back into his mouth. (They make a strange clunking sound as they settle down.)

Granny tries to change the subject. (Well, sort of.)

She's MADE her own biscuits.

Uh-oh.

"They are **packed** full of nuts, honey, and all kinds of other LOVELY stuff," she says.

Granny Mavis has very weird taste in food. So "other lovely stuff" could really be ANYTHING.

Here are a couple of her favorite "specials":

Granny's cheese and jam sandwiches

Grated chocolate on pasta

Dad says I'm allowed a homemade biscuit if I promise to brush my teeth afterward.

Granny arranges her "biscuits" on a plate and says, "Dig in!"

But her biscuits look a bit like . . .

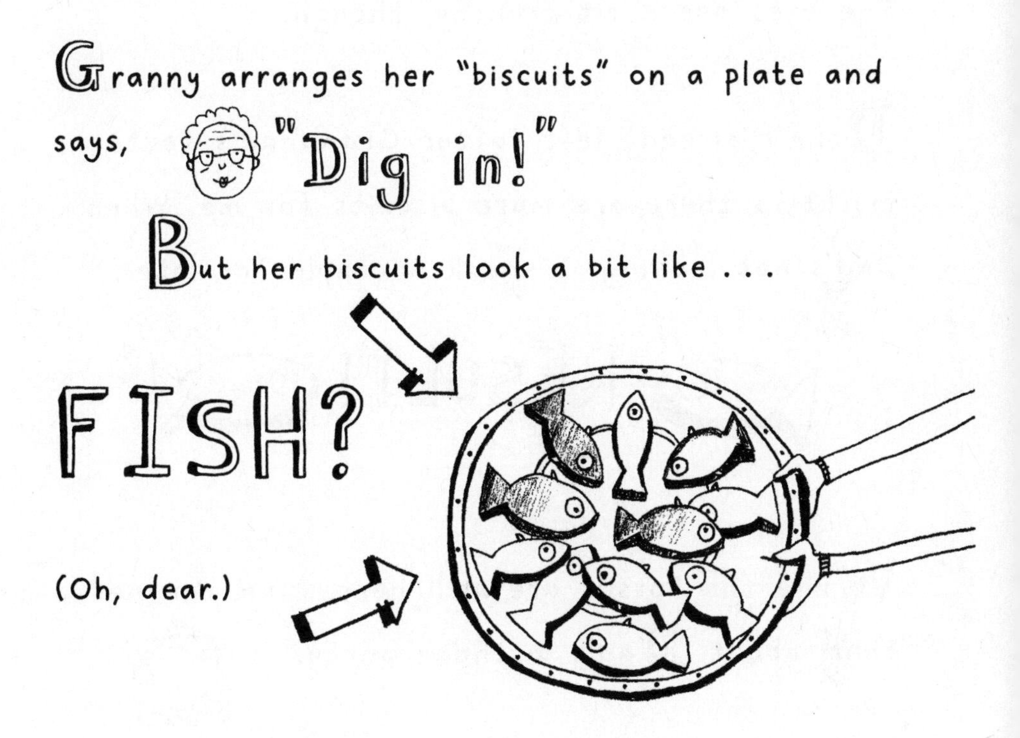

FISH?

(Oh, dear.)

"They're not fish flavored!" Granny assures me.

Phew. But they do have **BIG** staring eyes.

(I risk it . . . for a biscuit.)

Mmmmmm, surprisingly tasty for a fish biscuit.

The eyes are a bit crunchy, though.

Delia's already left (after Granddad's teeth trick) so there are more biscuits for me. When Dad's not looking, I sneak a couple for later.

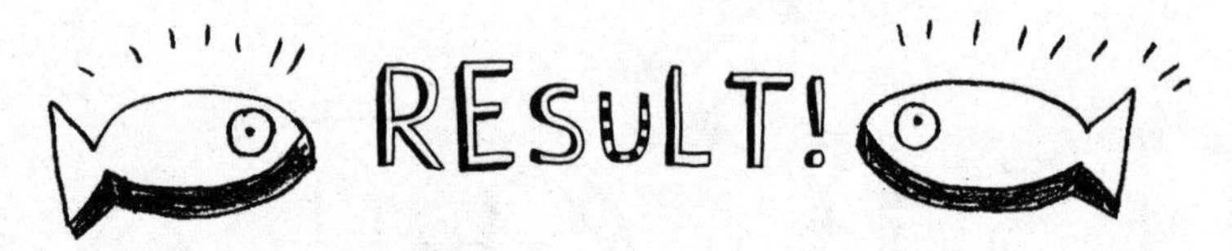

While the Fossils are still here, Mom reminds them about Dad's birthday party.

Dad is still not keen on having a party at ALL after last year.

So while he's grumbling and complaining, I remind everyone that it's MY birthday soon. And I'm VERY keen to have a PARTY with presents.

Granddad wonders what I'm interested in these days.
(Perfect time to drop "present hints.")

I am about to say DUDE 3 electric guitars, drawing stuff, that kind of thing.

When Mom **BUTTS** in with "Tom's REALLY interested in trees, aren't you, Tom?"

I am?

"Remember the wonderful piece of homework you did on trees?"

Errrrrrr.

I decide to take the praise while it's being handed to me because:

But just in case, I say,

"Trees are nice, but I don't want one for my birthday, thank you."

Granddad asks me about DOGZOMBIES, too.

(I'm very impressed he remembered my band's name!)

He says he has the PERFECT venue for us to play our VERY FIRST GIG . . . when we're ready.

"This place is always looking for new acts," Granddad says.

"Really?"

"Yes, you'll have a big audience of friendly people."

WOW, EXCELLENT! I can't wait to tell Derek. Then Granny offers me another biscuit, so I take it (to go with the other two I already have).

I have LOTS of good stuff to chat about with Derek now:

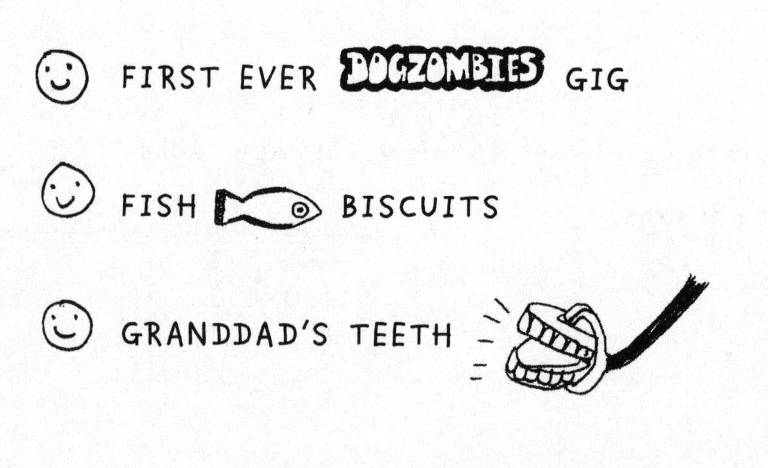

Over at Derek's house, he is **STILL** not very happy about being in the school band.

So I give him the **TWO** fish biscuits, which makes him laugh.

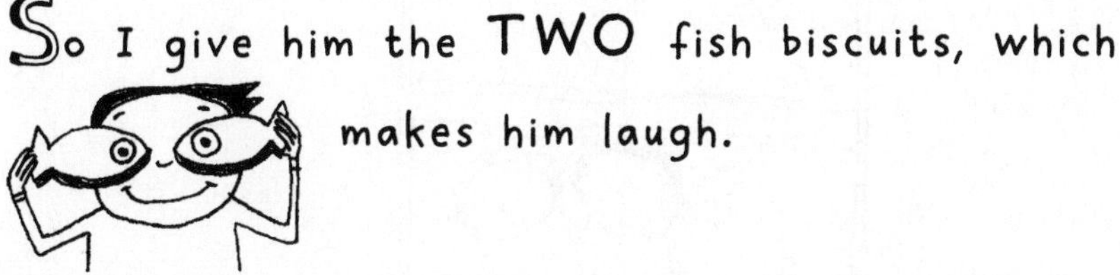

"Your granny's weird," he says, looking at the biscuit ⊙ ⊙ eyes.

"But they taste nice, though," he adds.

I'm telling Derek how **THE FOSSILS** are not always that bonkers and sometimes they're **REALLY** funny.

"Mostly they are just like really ordinary grandparents, honestly."

Derek says, "Are you sure about that?"

OK, maybe Derek has a point.

BYE.

. . . is doing that teacher thing of *leaning* on his desk and **Staring** at everyone.

He says he has got some very IMPORTANT news for us all.

(His idea of what's important is different from mine.)

For instance . . . DOGZOMBIES band auditions are important. I'm still not sure if I should say anything to AMY about them. I decide not to.

Not the right time. I notice that she's holding her pencil and tapping it on the desk (which is the sort of thing a drummer would do).

It's a good sign.

While I have been studying AMY'S drumming, Mr. Fullerman has gone ahead and made his

"IMPORTANT ANNOUNCEMENT."

I've missed it. Oh, well.

But then he asks me a question.

"Isn't that right . . . Tom?"

(This is why I prefer being at the BACK of the classroom, not at the front.)

I have NO idea what Mr. Fullerman is talking about, so I just agree with him.

"Great, well done, Tom. Does anyone else want to go, too?"

"No . . . OK, looks like it's just you, Tom. And Derek, too. Off you go. You'll be the first on the chart."

WHAT? THE FIRST? I have a horrible feeling about this. Well, at least I get to miss a lesson (I think?).

GOLD STAR AWARD CHART

CLASS 5F

MARK CLUMP	ROSS WHITE
BRAD GALLOWAY	SOLOMON STEWART
TOM GATES	PANSY BENNET
PAUL JOLLY	INDRANI HINDLE
LEROY LEWIS	FLORENCE MITCHELL
MARCUS MELDREW	JULIA MORTON
TREVOR PETERS	AMY PORTER
NORMAN WATSON	AMBER TULLEY GREEN

The GOOD NEWS is, I've got the FIRST GOLD STAR on the new Award Chart. Mr. Fullerman has given me a star for joining the school band. (Like I had a choice?)

Which is unexpected but nice.

The BAD news is, school band practice is on NOW and I'm the only one from 5F who's going. Oh well, at least I'm missing math lessons in class.

Question: How bad can a school band really be?

Answer: Worse than I thought.

Mr. Sprocket is delighted to see us.

Derek and I are not so delighted.

"Let me explain," Mr. Sprocket tells us. "This school band is different. We use instruments made from recycled rubbish.

We play new, modern music, too."

(Which just means no one has ever heard of it.)

"Not exactly DOGZOMBIES, is it?" I whisper to Derek.

Mr. Sprocket asks us to choose an "instrument." As there are NO guitars or keyboards, I pick the plastic-bottle-looking thing with chopsticks. Derek goes for the wooden box with elastic bands.

We do the best we can under the circumstances.

When I hit the bottles they are supposed to make different notes.

So far, mine only have two notes:

CLANG! and even LOUDER CLANG!

The other kids are more practiced ☹

than us—they are making it look easy (it's

not!).

We keep making mistakes.

I hit the bottles too hard.

Derek has snapped quite a few of

his elastic bands. PING

Then I break a

chopstick and half of it flies through

the air.

School band is not going well.

Even Mr. Sprocket looks a little weary.

One kid puts his hand up.

"Sir, why are they in our band?"

"OUR BAND?" I thought it was a school band?

Mr. Sprocket tells him to put his hand down because we'll be fine,

after one or two more rehearsals.

"More like one or two HUNDRED."

I can hear more kids laughing now.

I'm going to HAVE to think of a really EXCELLENT excuse to get out of this band.

It's been an Awful practice.

Derek agrees. "That was embarrassing," he says.

Then I notice where the other half of my chopstick has landed.

I nudge Derek. "No, THAT'S embarrassing."

We leave quickly, before he notices.

Whoops

Outside the classroom, Amy and Florence are walking past.

"Is this *your* new band, Tom?" Amy asks.

"No way," I say. "This is the school band. It's a bit rubbish, really." The kids in the school band hear me and are not happy. ☹

"We're not rubbish. YOU'RE the one who's rubbish."

"And so's your friend."

"We'd be ten times better if you weren't in the school band."

(They have a point.)

GREAT. Now Amy and Florence think that we're hopeless. I'm just about to EXPLAIN to them that we play

REAL instruments in **DOGZOMBIES**,

but Amy and Florence have gone.

"This **school band** could **RUIN** our

reputation . . . if we had one," Derek says.

It's true.

Today we've been a bit:

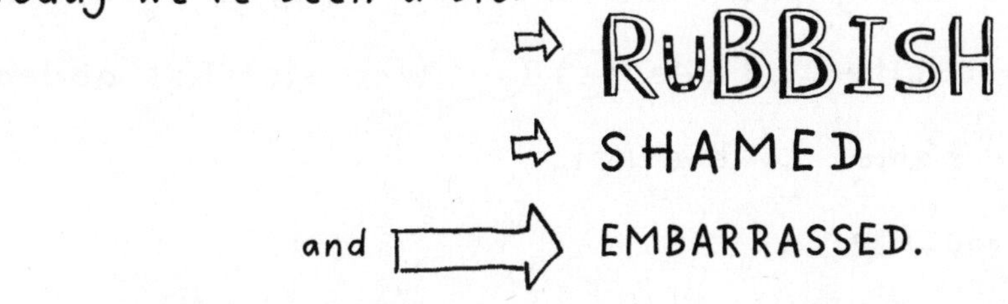

⇨ **RUBBISH**

⇨ SHAMED

and ⇨ EMBARRASSED.

Derek and I decide we have to get out of

the school band, one way or another.

It's the most important thing to do ever.

Until I find a spare wafer in my pocket.

YEAH!

The poster has been up for a few days and we're doing the auditions TOMORROW, so I am very excited to see who else has added their names to the list.

Let me see....

HANG ON!

AND

FLORENCE MITCHELL'S

names have been CROSSED OUT?

What's going on? Who's done that?

So far the only *REAL* person who's coming to the audition is: HYPERACTIVE

NORMAN WATSON.

I take down the poster and go and find Amy quickly.

Stan, the school janitor, is holding open the door for some kids. I can see Amy and Florence in front of me. So I

RUSH past everyone, saying,

"EMERGENCY!

EMERGENCY!

EMERGENCY!"

Which gets their  attention.

I catch up with Amy and Florence and show them the poster.

"Look at what SOMEBODY HAS done! Can you believe they've actually CROSSED BOTH your names OFF from the audition! What kind of an IDIOT would ruin your chances of being in DOGZOMBIES by doing something as STUPID as that?"

Then Amy says,

(Oh . . . I wasn't expecting that.)

Florence says, "We don't play drums, Tom."

"And we didn't write our names on your poster. Sorry," Amy adds.

"Does that mean you won't be auditioning, then?" Just checking.

Janitor Stan is listening to our conversation.

"Hey! Looking for a drummer? Well, look no further!"

Stan thinks he's funny. Groan.

He pretends to do a drumroll and cymbal crash.

(Which is rubbish.)

The door slowly closes while Stan continues to air drum.

I'm trying not to look fed up.

"You wouldn't want us in your band, Tom," Florence says.

"We'd be **ROTTEN**," Amy adds.

"Worse than Stan?" I say.

(We can still hear Stan's keys jangling in the background.)

Amy suspects whoever wrote the SILLY names on the poster also wrote their names on it, too.

Good point.

"See if you can match the handwriting on the poster to anyone in our class," Amy suggests.

"That's genius!" I say. (She's so smart.)

Whoever wanted to mess up the audition poster is probably feeling pretty pleased with themselves right now.

I'm searching the classroom for ANYONE who seems slightly more smug than usual. . . .

Extreme close-up

Surprise, surprise. . . .

It **WAS** Marcus who wrote on the poster. He admits it.

He says, "You didn't actually think Amy and Florence wanted to be in your band, did you?" Ha! Ha! Ha! he laughs. (He's so annoying.)

Mr. Fullerman has marked all our REVIEW homework and is handing them back to us.

"Well done, Tom, excellent work," he says.

Marcus doesn't get a mention.

(I did my homework quickly, so this is very good news.)

Good work, Tom.

Your special interest in trees will be very useful on the field trip.

Well done.

3 merits and ONE GOLD STAR.

THAT'S why Mr. Fullerman thought I was interested in TREES.

I'll show this to Mom and Dad, who might give me a REWARD.

I could try the "good parenting" line again?

Worth a go. . . .

Right now I enjoy collecting my

SECOND GOLD STAR.

2 merits = 1 GOLD STAR.

Whoever gets the MOST stars at the end of the term wins "spectacular prizes." (So Mr. Fullerman tells us.)

I suspect the prizes will be things like pencil cases and school tea towels.

NOT very spectacular at all.

But as I am in the lead with two stars . . . I don't care.

I leave my book open so MARCUS can see my

MERITS

AND GOLD STARS.

Sadly, nobody else (REAL) has put their names down for our audition.

Looks like it's ONLY NORMAN coming now. I don't think his audition will take too long.

Derek hopes someone else will turn up . . . other than just his dad. Who keeps popping in.

Anyone here yet?

Derek sends him away.

I remind Derek that my granddad has

already booked DOGZOMBIES' FIRST-EVER GIG!

"We can still do it, even if we don't have a drummer," I say.

(That's plan B, in case no one turns up.)

"Granddad says we'll be in front of a nice, friendly crowd."

"BRILLIANT." Derek is trying to be positive.

"We could become the NEXT

DUDE3," I say. How cool would that be?

Then Norman turns up, which brings us right back down to earth.

He's being his usual TWITCHY self. "Hey, Norman, just relax and play anything you want to," I tell him.

(We're not expecting too much from him.)

"Bit nervous," he says as he knocks over another drum.

It's not a great start.

The noise gives Derek's dad an excuse to COME in AGAIN to see what we're getting up to (like he doesn't already know).

I'm really hoping that Norman's drumming is better than his swimming . . . but so far, it's not looking good.

Norman settles down (a bit).

Then he starts to play.

And we're all in for a MASSIVE SURPRISE....

OK, he is a bit wild....

When he's finished playing, we tell Norman he's "IN THE BAND!" Which sets him off again.

Norman is much better at playing than we are.

"We might have to practice more,"

I say to Derek.

"You'll sound like a proper band with Norman drumming!" Mr. Fingle tells us.

Then he adds,

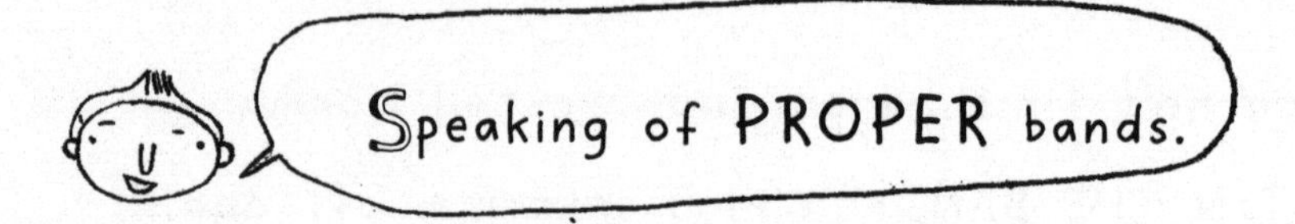

(Uh-oh.) We haven't had a chance to

Norman about Mr. Fingle's little

He's already rummaging in his record collection.

"Have you ever heard of a band called

THE WHO, Norman?"

"Who?" Norman says.

"NO, THE WHO,"

Mr. Fingle repeats.

Then Norman asks, "Who are the Who, then?"

Which is really confusing.

Derek wants his dad to STOP chatting.

"Not now, Dad, PLEASE!"

(But it's too late.)

"Only one of the BEST BANDS in the whole world ever!" he says as he proudly shows Norman the record.

"This is a CLASSIC. You must listen to it . . . right NOW!"

Norman says, "Ok, sure!"

Then jumps up just a little bit too quickly to take a look at the album.

The record flies out of its sleeve, HIGH in the air, then lands on the ground.
It rolls across the floor,
through some dust,
spins a bit, then comes to a stop.

Mr. Fingle is  FREAKING out that his record has been SCRATCHED and ruined.

"Don't PANIC,

I'll FETCH IT!" he shouts.

Really, REALLY LOUDLY.

SO loudly that Rooster (Derek's dog) hears the word FETCH and runs in from the garden. He grabs the record in his teeth, then disappears out the door. Followed quickly by Mr. Fingle.

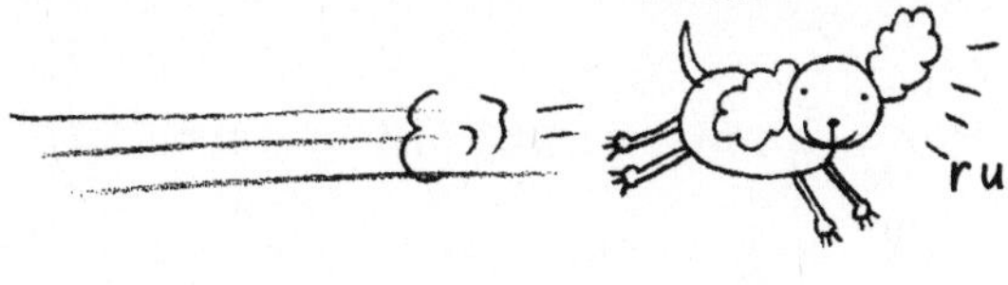

Derek says he's never seen his dad run so fast.

"It must be a really good album," Norman says.

"And Rooster has very good taste in music," I add.

The audition is over now, so we watch Mr. Fingle chase Rooster all around the house.

When I get home,
this letter from my school
has turned up.

From: Oakfield School

To: Mr. and Mrs. Gates
24 Castle St
EGP 1963

I'm wondering WHAT I've done NOW? So I open it carefully and take a sneaky look.

PHEW! Just a reminder about the school field trip and a special Clothes List.

(Nothing important, then.)

I'm LATE

for the field trip due to:

1. Forgetting about the field trip.

2. Forgetting I still had my pajama bottoms on as I left for school.

I run back to get changed.

Delia sees me and is her usual helpful self.

I only **just** make it to school on time.

LATE AGAIN, TOM?

Mr. Fullerman and the whole class are waiting for me outside. For some strange reason Mr. Fullerman is dressed like a

jungle explorer?

Solid is there and wearing very impressive waterproof boots.

I ask him if Mr. Fullerman is looking for

BUGS or TIGERS?

He laughs **loudly** and Mr. Fullerman STARES at me . . . then at my feet. (Uh-oh.)

Apparently I'm wearing

Inappropriate footwear

And I might have to wear the

SPARE BOOTS!

(NOT the SPARE BOOTS.

No! No!)

The "SPARE" stuff is mostly MANKY bits of lost property that no one wants (like these).

(I hope Mr. Fullerman forgets about my shoes.)

MRS. Mumble is on the trip with us. She's holding the bag of "spare stuff."

"For emergencies," she tells me cheerily.

"Or people with inappropriate footwear," Marcus adds.

I ignore him.

Norman is still very overexcited about being in DOGZOMBIES.

He keeps jumping around and using his magnifying glass to LOOM up to people with one big EYE. (It's getting on everyone's nerves.)

Marcus is getting on my nerves.

"Didn't you read the field trip clothes list?" he asks me.

"SHHHHH," I say.

It will be ALL Marcus's fault if I have to wear the SPARE BOOTS.

Mr. Fullerman gets distracted when Norman looms up to Julia Morton once too often.

We all have to "PAY ATTENTION" to the safety talk about things that could

and

BITE.

"You must behave SENSIBLY."

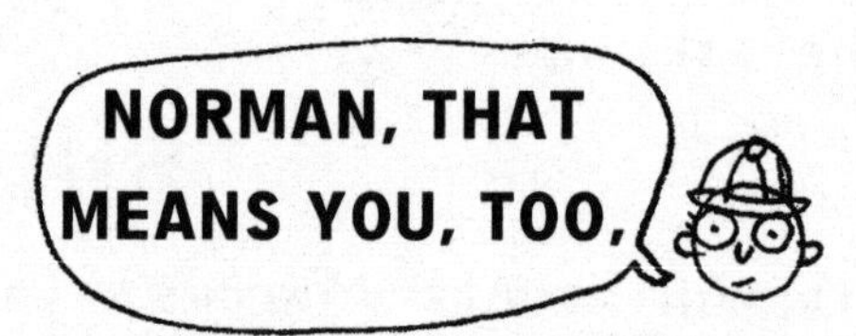

Mr. Fullerman says.

We set off with Mr. Fullerman at the front and Mrs. Mumble at the back to make sure no one dawdles behind.

Don't dawdle

We're not going far, just to the local field.

When we get there we are put into groups and have to go off and identify as many different types of plants, leaves, and TREES as we can.

"You should be good at this, Tom, you know a lot about trees," Mr. Fullerman says.

Great, now my group thinks I'm some kind of WEIRD TREE EXPERT. (I'm not.)

Instead I just make stuff up, which seems to work.

I'm really looking forward to using the BUG CATCHERS we've been given.

Pansy Bennet has already found an

ENORMOUS

spider.

Leroy Lewis is studying a bug that ROLLS up in a ball.

Mark Clump is catching EVERYTHING.

Ants, bugs, spiders, frogs—the lot.

I spot a really brightly colored beetle. I've never seen one like that before.

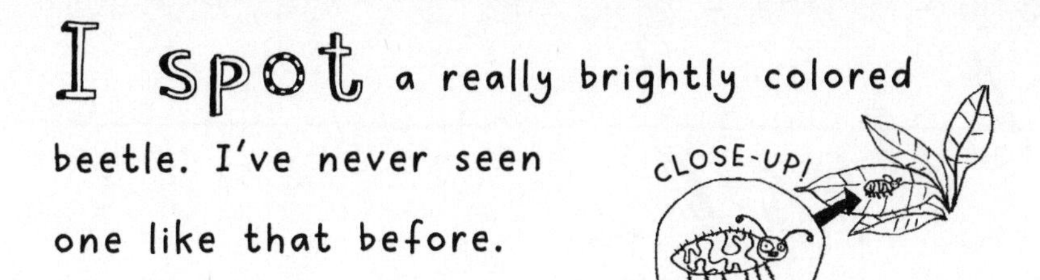

I sneak up really slowly. THIS bug looks AMAZING, I might even get THREE merits (and one GOLD STAR☆) for discovering it.

I lower my bug catcher over the bug carefully. . . .

Easy does it. . . .

Marcus suddenly

traps it in **HIS** bug catcher.

"THAT'S MINE," he says.

(I really hope it bites him or stings him . . . or both.)

MINE!
Irritating or what?

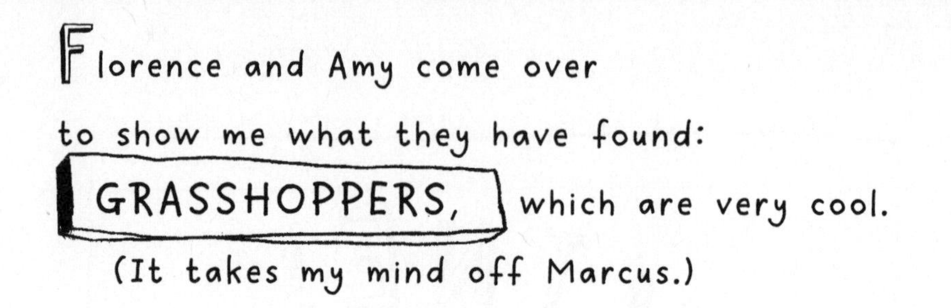

Florence and Amy come over

to show me what they have found:

GRASSHOPPERS, which are very cool.

(It takes my mind off Marcus.)

Amy wonders how the audition

went "with ONLY Norman turning up?"

"He was BRILLIANT," I say.

"Really?" Florence doesn't sound convinced.

"Aren't you worried about Norman being in the band?" Amy asks.

"No, not really," I say. "Norman can be a bit, you know . . ."

"Bonkers," Florence adds.

So I tell them,

"You'd be surprised. Norman's actually a REALLY GREAT drummer."

"What about all the crazy things he does?" Amy says.

"Norman's not THAT bad. Honestly, when was the last time you saw him do something REALLY silly?" I add.

Just as Norman turns up holding

TWO green caterpillars

under his nose.

(Not now, Norman. . . . Groan.)

We are sitting on the grass eating our packed lunches when SOLID (who looks a bit miserable) shows me the only thing he's found so far.

I think it's half a dead bug. . . .

half bug

It is half a dead bug.

"I'll help you find something else," I say.

So Solid FLICKS the dead bug away.

(Which probably wasn't the best idea.)

The bug flies through the air and lands right on Julia Morton's sandwich.

Julia SCREAMS and says she feels sick now.

Mrs. Mumble assures her that the bug probably fell from the tree.

(Me and Solid keep quiet.)

Unlike MARCUS, who tells Julia that there is a very good reason she has only HALF a dead bug on her sandwich.

"What's that, then?" Julia asks.

"You must have EATEN the other half already."

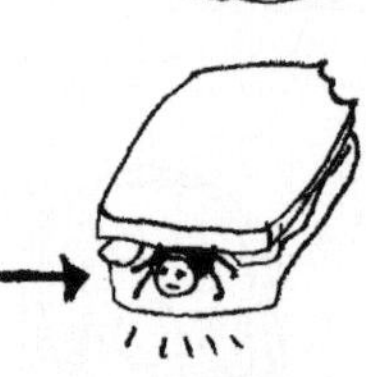

The whole class go "UGGGGHHHHHHHHhh!"

Julia turns green. (She's the same color as the grass now.)

Marcus is laughing and being particularly irritating today.

Mr. Fullerman tells everyone to **"Calm down!"**

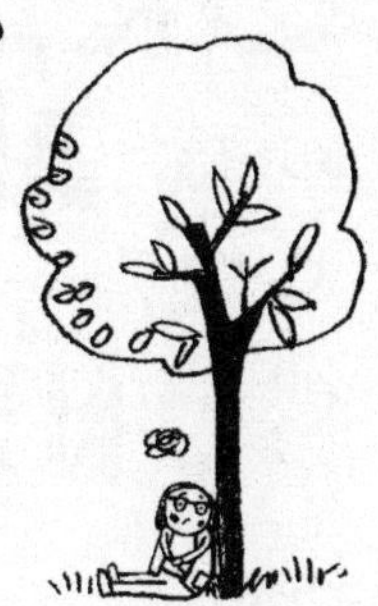

He lets Julia "recover" by sitting under a tree. Then takes the rest of the class down to the pond to carry on looking for creatures.

OK, now I see why I needed to wear boots. SOLID has already SUNK down into the MUD and has to be pulled out by Mrs. Mumble. (Who's a LOT stronger than she looks.)

Mrs. Mumble tells me to keep clear of the MUD "in those shoes."

Then Marcus adds, "He should be wearing the SPARE BOOTS, Mrs. Mumble."

SHUT UP, MARCUS! I wish he'd sink down in the mud.

Mr. Fullerman calls us all over to see what he's been collecting in the bucket. Amongst all the SLIME and WEEDS are some tiny little fish and other interesting things.

"Take turns looking. . . . Don't push,"

Mr. Fullerman says.

(Marcus is pushing now.) It's tricky to see exactly what's in there. SOLID thinks he saw a "WATER SNAKE!"

"You can all see. . . . Be patient,"

Mr. Fullerman tells us.

Then he asks Mark Clump and Amber Tulley Green to help carry the bucket up the grass.

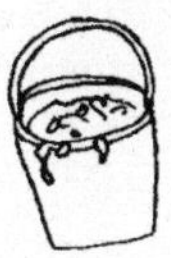

Norman's not great at being patient and can't wait. He hears Solid say "WATER SNAKE" and gets really excited. Then accidentally *T R I P S* over a twig and falls on Amber.

Who lets go of the bucket.

Mark Clump holds on with one hand.

Until a BIG FROG

POPS out of his pocket.

(He'd forgotten about the frog.)

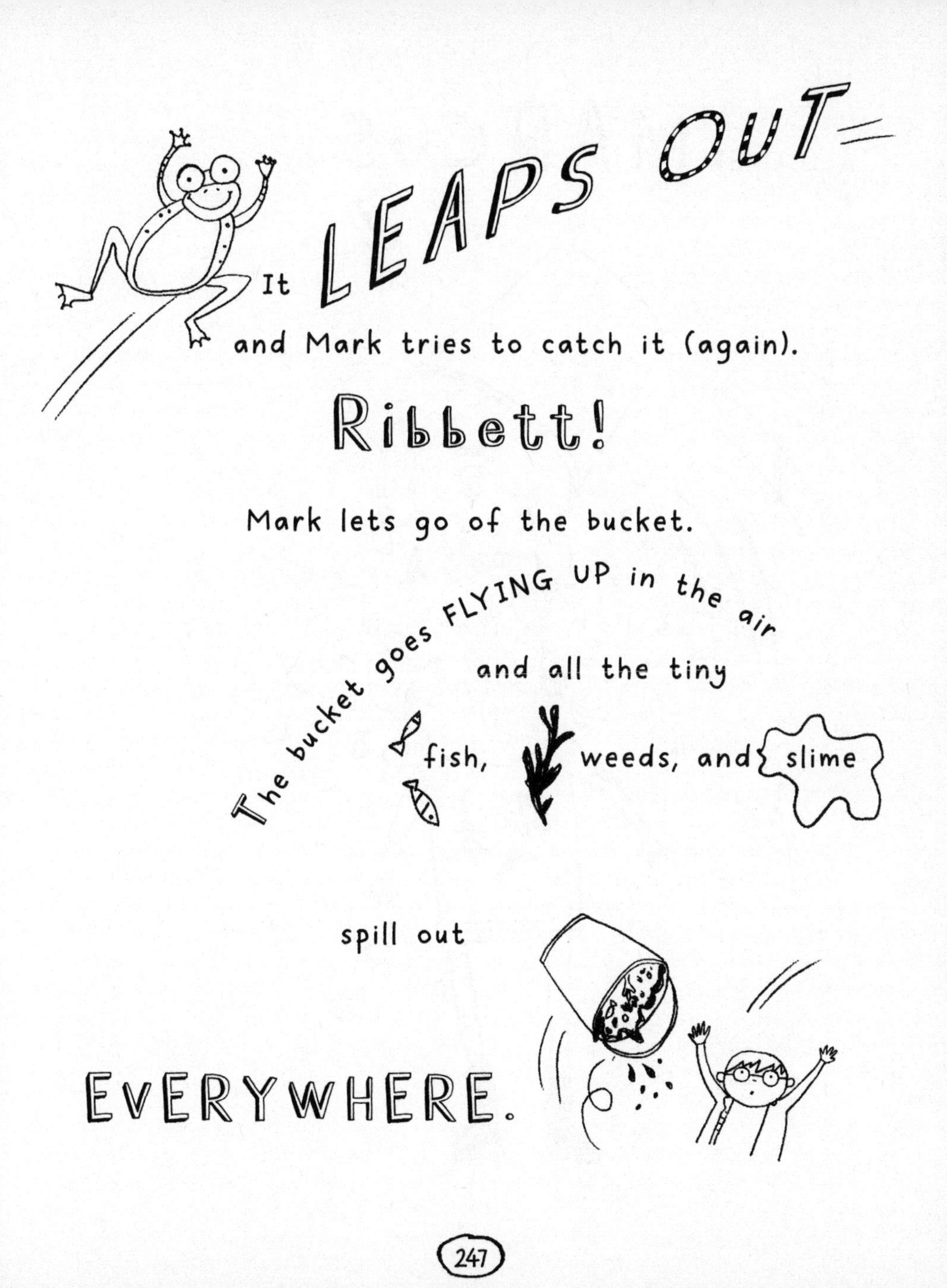
It LEAPS OUT
and Mark tries to catch it (again).
Ribbett!
Mark lets go of the bucket.
The bucket goes FLYING UP in the air
and all the tiny
fish, weeds, and slime
spill out
EVERYWHERE.

ALL OVER MARCUS.

(Turns out there wasn't a water snake in the bucket after all. Just lots and lots of slime.) Marcus is not happy. Solid has cheered up, though. Mrs. Mumble comes to the rescue with a towel. She says:

"Don't panic, I've got just the thing for this kind of

Mr. Fullerman and the rest of the class scoop up any fish or creatures from the ground and take them back to the pond, while Mrs. Mumble helps Marcus.

She says,

"Thank GOODNESS we brought the SPARE CLOTHES . . .

and the SPARE BOOTS!"

(I agree. ☺)

Marcus has to wear them all the way back

to school. Which **inspires** me to draw some of the bugs and creatures I COULD HAVE found on the field trip.

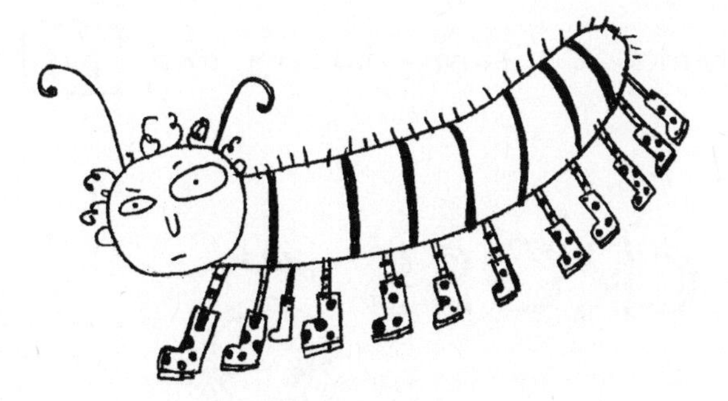

Worth at least five merits, I think?

Dad's Birthday

Everyone's coming to our house for Dad's birthday party, which means Mom is a LOT more stressed than usual. She keeps saying things like

"Take it upstairs!" and

"Rubbish outside!"

Delia thinks it's funny to try and put ME outside.

Mom gets CROSS

and says that we had **BOTH** better behave when guests arrive

The whole house is all

CLEAN and TIDY.

Until the Fingles turn up early with their dog, Rooster. He's got really muddy paws.

Rooster isn't in the house for very long thanks to Mom.

Derek gives Dad his present. (I can guess what it is from its shape.) ☺

Dad's DELIGHTED. He's already discussing with Mr. Fingle "classic albums" and "great bands of our day."

(Yawn.)

I give Dad my present before he gets too carried away chatting.

It's a T-shirt with my drawing on the front.

Dad LOVES it!

He says I've gone to a LOT of trouble.

Actually it was Mom who put it on a T-shirt.

But I'm happy to take the praise.

Thank you. Thank you.

Dad wants to wear it straightaway.

"IT FITS?" Mom says because she thought it might be a bit snug.

(Which doesn't go down well with Dad.)

Derek says that DOGZOMBIES should have T-shirts, too. Which is an

EXCELLENT idea.

When Uncle Kevin, Auntie Alice, and the cousins turn up, they are all wearing

VERY *fancy* clothes.

Dad wonders if they are going to another party afterward?

Uncle Kevin says, "It's important to make an effort when you're invited out."

(He's looking at Dad like he's a bit scruffy.)

So Dad tells him that I made the T-shirt as a present.

"Tom's so talented—isn't it great?"

Which makes Delia do "I'm going to be sick" signs behind Dad's back.

I ignore her and AGREE with Dad, that I am a GENIUS. . . . It's true.

Uncle Kevin says, "Well done, Tom."

And Dad's happy . . .

until Auntie Alice gives him their present.

It's a book called

Uncle Kevin says,

"We saw this and thought of you."

Auntie Alice adds, "It was recommended for men of your age."

Dad says "Thanks!" but he doesn't look

THAT pleased.

arrive in their usual

. Granny has brought one of her cakes. (Well, I think it's a cake; you never know with Granny.)

cake

I'm guessing Delia FORGOT to buy Dad a present. Because she's just given him . . . a pair of her OLD sunglasses?

Dad puts them on and says, "Thanks, Delia, I look JUST like you now!"

Which is not really true because Dad is SMILING.

Mom tells me I have to

look after Derek and your cousins.

(This means "keep out of trouble.")

Everything's going well until all the good snacks run out.

Then the cousins announce that

they have brought over

so we can ALL finish watching it.

"Let's watch it NOW,"

they say.

(Let's not.)

Derek looks keen to see it, but I want to avoid hiding behind cushions AGAIN.

QUICKLY I suggest, "We should play a few jokes instead."

Which turns out to be a BRILLIANT IDEA.

The whoopee cushion
works well
on Delia.
And Auntie
Alice, too.

Putting me inside a LARGE box as an "EXTRA present" for Dad was INSPIRED.

I SPRING out shouting

Dad laughs but Uncle
Kevin's not smiling much,
because I've accidentally

knocked a bowl of crisps all over his fancy bow tie.

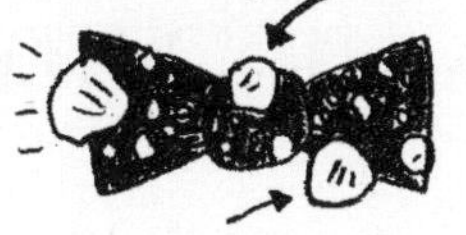

Mom **AND** Uncle Kevin are GLARING at me. When Granny comes to my rescue by bringing in Dad's birthday cake . . .

which is slightly unusual?

"It's a delicious **vegetable** cake," she says.

(Ummm, it doesn't look so delicious to me.)

We all wish Dad a very happy birthday.
Luckily, he thinks the BIRTHDAY RHYME
I made up is funny.

A GREAT birthday to YOU
You're ONE HUNDRED and TWO
You've lost all your hair now
And your TEETH are brand-new. ☺

Dad blows out his candles and calls me a
"cheeky monkey."
Uncle Kevin jokes that if we run out of breath
we might need a fire
extinguisher for all those candles.
Ha. Ha.

The cousins dig into the cake
first. (No surprise there.)
It MUST taste better than it looks.

"This Sunday?

That's a bit soon, isn't it?" I say.

Granddad says it's all booked. So we'd better get practicing. Which is a good point because we still only know a few songs.

"Besides, if you don't come and play, I'll be **FORCED** to entertain everyone with my ONE VERY special party trick," Granddad tells us.

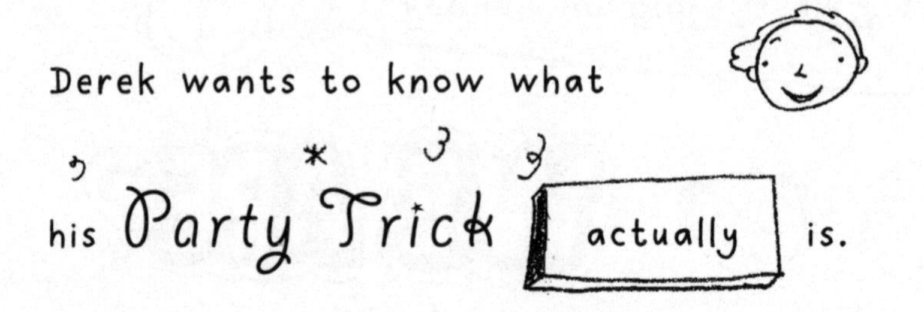

Derek wants to know what his *Party Trick* actually is.

(I'm not sure what it is either.)

OK,

just remembered.

Meanwhile . . . the cousins STILL want me to see the film.

(I'd rather watch Granddad take his teeth out again.) But it's too late, they are sitting in front of the TV waiting for me to join them.

MYSTERIOUSLY . . . the remote control goes MISSING.

(I've hidden it.)

Remote control is MISSING

I tell them that the TV is STUCK on this channel. Which is showing a program on . . . VAMPIRES. (That's lucky.)

I leave them to it. The cousins are VERY happy until Auntie Alice and Uncle Kevin come to take them home.

Which turns out to be a **lot** sooner

than expected due to Uncle Kevin hurting his back. "I knew dancing was a mistake," he says.

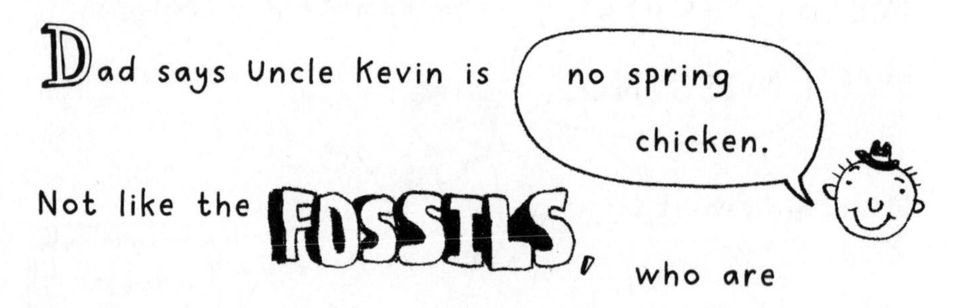

Dad says Uncle Kevin is no spring chicken.

Not like the FOSSILS, who are having a great time making everyone join in their CONGA line. They dance all around the house and into the garden, too. It's slightly embarrassing (but fun).

At least Dad looks like he's enjoying himself this year.

Unlike Delia.

The Special ASSEMBLY

Get this . . .

Derek is not in school this morning because he's sprained his ankle

I have to go in on my own, which is FINE until I get to school and overhear Mr. Keen talking to Mr. Fullerman about the

OH! NO! What with Dad's birthday and everything, I have completely forgotten all about the *special assembly* and playing in the school band!

(DEREK picked a good day for a dodgy ankle.)

I'm trying to avoid Mr. Keen AGAIN, until I can think of an EXCELLENT excuse to get myself OUT of this sticky situation. It's bad enough playing "instruments" (bottles with chopsticks). But doing it without Derek will be too embarrassing for me.

What to do?

I walk very *SLOWLY* into class to give myself time to think.

Marcus is walking in front of me. He starts LIMPING when he sees me.

"The dog bite scar?"

Marcus says. "It still hurts." This gives me an idea.

(Thanks, Marcus, for a change.)

DISASTER! I am STRUCK DOWN with a terrible DEAD ARM ache.

Mr. Fullerman wonders how this could have happened **SO** suddenly?

I explain how my older sister, DELIA, pushed me out of the house and how **she** MUST have sprained my "instrument-playing arm **VERY** badly."

"It's **AGONY**," I say.

I do some extra VERY LOUD groaning during attendance, which I think helps. Mr. Fullerman sends me to the nurse's office—again.

I moan a bit more (OK, a lot more, for extra effect on the way out).

Mrs. Mumble tells me to sit in the nurse's office and wait for a bit.

Nurse's Office

UNFORTUNATELY

I miss **ALL** of the special assembly and playing in the school band, too.

RESULT!

Once everything is safely over, I make a remarkable recovery.

My arm is fine now . . .

see?

Ta-da!

It's a MIRACLE.

It's safe to go back to class.

I just have to avoid Mr. Keen for the rest of the day, which I manage to do with the help of:

I can't avoid Mr. Fullerman, though. He calls me over for a **"quick chat."** (I think he's slightly suspicious about my instant recovery from arm ache.)

Mr. Fullerman says,

"Such a shame you missed the special assembly, Tom."

(Not really.)

"Glad your arm is better . . . so quickly, too?"

(Uh-oh.)

I tell Mr. Fullerman my arm feels absolutely FINE now. And THAT'S when I notice the book under Mr. Fullerman's arm.

IT's a book on TREES.

(Which looks VERY familiar?)

Mr. Fullerman hands me a note he's written about my **REVIEW** HOMEWORK. The one I did so quickly.

About TREES. . . .

It's all coming back to me now. . . . Whoops.

Tom,

Imagine my surprise when I came across this book on TREES and realized I had read the back somewhere before?

Your REVIEW HOMEWORK on trees.

I am very disappointed in you, Tom. Copying is NOT something you should be doing and is a serious offense!

I want a new review done quickly or another letter goes home to your parents.

Mr. Fullerman

Point taken.

TREES:
This book aims to give you many interesting facts on trees. From where the largest tree in the world is, to how much food and shelter a tree can provide for wildlife.

Did you know that trees are the longest-living organisms on Earth?

And that one acre of trees takes away nearly 2.6 tons of carbon dioxide each year?

The world's oldest trees are thought to be 5,000-year-old BRISTLECONE pines that are in the U.S.A. There are so many benefits that trees bring to our cities and many communities. They provide beauty and shade. Trees can make you feel serene and peaceful.

I hope the information in this book will inspire you to enjoy trees and plant more of them.

By A. Corn

BAD NEWS

Mr. Fullerman has REMOVED one of my GOLD STARS from my chart until I hand in the new piece of review homework. **"LAST CHANCE, Tom,"** he tells me. I can see that Marcus has a LOT more gold stars than I do. Which is annoying.

Mr. Fullerman even gave him a gold star for **"collecting an unusual beetle."**

Which was REALLY irritating

because I saw it first!

But he's WAY ahead of the whole class, even Amy. How's that happened?

Marcus is a sneaky so and so. Which makes me wonder if he's been

CHEATING?

On the way home, I am discussing my suspicions about Marcus with Derek, who wants to get some fruit chews from the shop.

And guess who's already there?

We say "Hi" but he's too busy looking for something . . . and it's NOT sweets.

Derek picks out a few fruit chews while I read this week's copy of **ROCK WEEKLY**. (I'm off sweets due to my dodgy tooth . . . for now.)

When we leave the shop I notice that MARCUS is standing in the section that has paper, envelopes, and . . . stickers.

"That's odd," I say to Derek as we leave the shop.

"I wonder what Marcus was buying?"

He's DEFINITELY up to something.

So we decide to take a peek through the shop window.

Sure enough . . .

there's Marcus buying what looks like a very

LARGE box OF GOLD STAR STICKERS.

I knew it! Marcus has been adding his own stars to the chart. Catching him in the act won't be easy, though. I will need VERY BEADY EYES like Mr. Fullerman's.

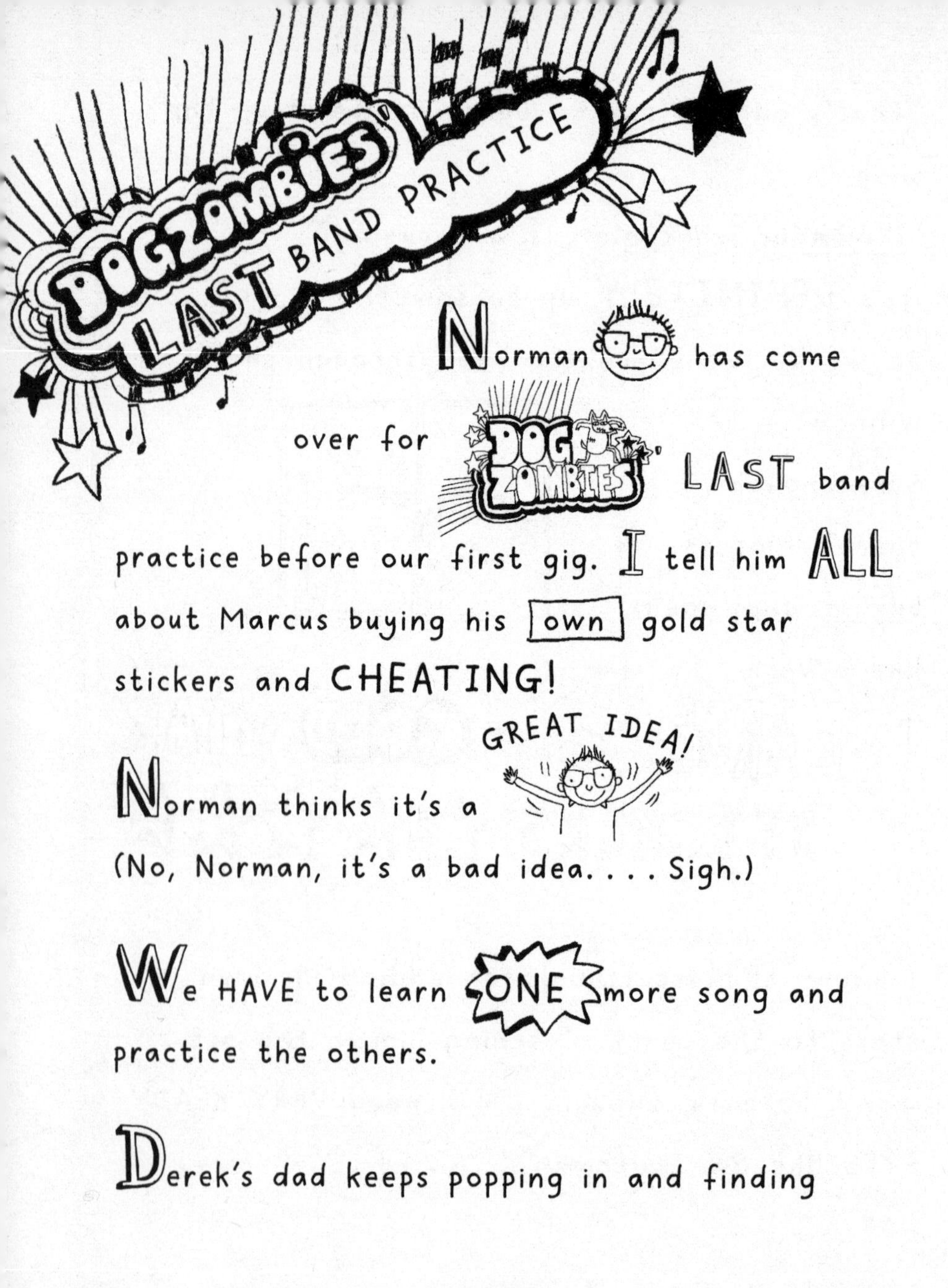

Norman has come over for DOGZOMBIES' LAST band practice before our first gig. I tell him ALL about Marcus buying his own gold star stickers and CHEATING!

Norman thinks it's a GREAT IDEA!

(No, Norman, it's a bad idea. . . . Sigh.)

We HAVE to learn ONE more song and practice the others.

Derek's dad keeps popping in and finding

excuses to come and see us rehearse.

Everything OK?

Even though we have ALL learned

NOT to CHAT to Mr. Fingle about music

(unless you have TEN HOURS

to spare), right now we *NEED* his help.

Derek asks if he could suggest a good song for us to learn . . . today?

"Leave it to me, lads . . ."

(He's VERY excited.) He takes out a Deep Purple record.

We work hard with Mr. Fingle's help.

So DOGZOMBIES (that's us) has managed to add

to our gig list.

RESULT!

Norman already knows how to play it, and me and Derek try our best. The singing is tricky, especially when Mr. Fingle keeps joining in.

Let's hope we've done enough to keep Granddad's teeth FIRMLY in his mouth on Sunday.

Now that we've finished practicing, Derek is looking for the last of the fruit chews he saved as a treat. But he can't find them anywhere. I haven't eaten them.

But I think I know who has. . . .

It's a warning to us that

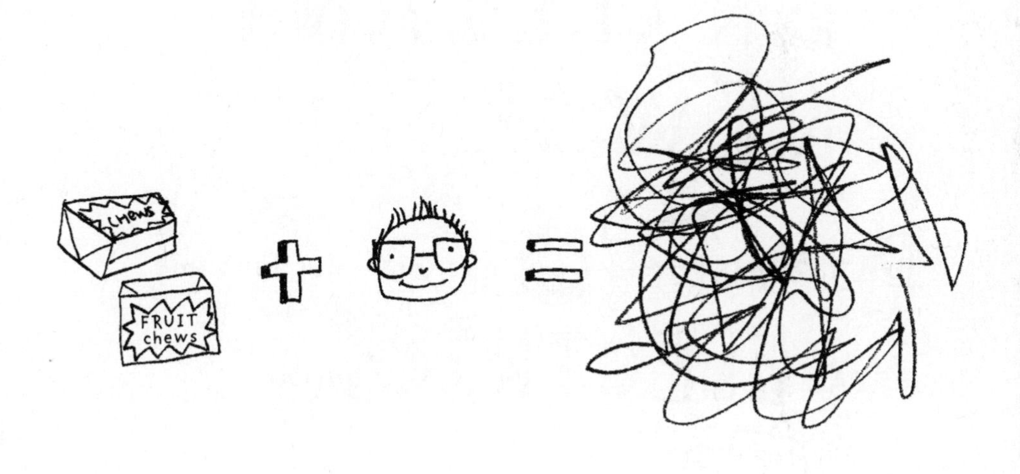

BRILLIANT NEWS!

ED

Delia's boyfriend has actually lent me a REAL ELECTRIC guitar and an amp so I can play REALLY LOUDLY!

From the look on Delia's face, it's all working fine.

Dad says he's coming along as our

"ROADIE" to help set everything up. He's taking it all very seriously

(and he's made a long list).

Mom is busy with her camera.

While we have our first **BAND PHOTO** done,

Dad keeps doing

embarrassing rock-star poses.

Me and Derek are a bit **nervous.**

Norman is always so jumpy that you can't

tell if he is or not.

I have a lucky escape when Mom tries to

HUG me and wishes the band

good luck.

Delia is her usual charming self.

Dad has packed the car and stuffed the roof rack. Then we're off to meet Granddad. It's only when we're driving that I realize . . .

we have NO idea where exactly we're playing our first gig.

Dad says it will be a NICE BIG

SURPRISE

for us!

LEAFY GREEN
OLD FOLKS' HOME

"LEAFY GREEN OLD FOLKS' HOME?" I say.

Granddad says they'll LOVE us.

"I have lots of friends here who are looking forward to seeing you!"

REALLY?

"And it won't matter how loud you play or if you make any mistakes because MOST of the audience are a bit hard of hearing. Just have some fun!"

Great. I'm wondering just how much "fun" the old folks are really going to have listening to us?

Pardon?

Granddad has put up **LOTS** of posters around the home already. He's now telling everyone that I'm his grandson and that **DOGZOMBIES** is going to be

So they must come and see us.

(Thanks, Granddad.)

We have to wait for the lounge to be **FREE** before we can set up.

And I manage to avoid a potential disaster by keeping Norman away from the tray of biscuits. PHEW!

We've got quite a crowd now, but it takes a while for the old folks to get settled and comfy.

When Granddad introduces us, he says,

"Can you all hear me back there?"

Which sets off everyone saying "Pardon?" "Eh?" "Pardon?"

Never mind, we can play loudly.

Then Granddad says, "Let's give a WARM LEAFY GREEN welcome to the amazing . . . DOGZOMBIES."

And it's over to us to start with a rousing rendition of "Delia's a Weirdo" (which seems to all go down well).

Our first-ever gig was . . . OK. Not brilliant . . . just OK. (Room for improvement.) We made a few mistakes, but no one seemed to notice.

All in all, we had a good time, Norman didn't go too wild, and Granddad's teeth stayed firmly in place the whole time, which is a good sign, I think? And I heard a few people singing

"Delia's a WEIRDO"

when we left.

Result! ☺

Granddad says there are a lot of other old folks' homes we could play. "Everyone has to start somewhere!" he reminds us.

True.

(I wonder where DUDE 3 played their first gig?)

Back at home I'm reading Delia's copy of ROCK WEEKLY and imagining that DOGZOMBIES is being interviewed by the magazine about the success of their first-ever gig (and other important music matters).

OLDIES ROCK OUT TO DOGZOMBIES' FIRST GIG!

Rock Weekly: So, Tom, who are your INFLUENCES for DOGZOMBIES?

Tom: That's a very good question. All sorts of things, really. DUDE3 is a huge influence. And I'm often inspired to write songs by VERY irritating family members.

RW: "Delia's a Weirdo"?

Tom: I couldn't have said it better myself.

RW: Why did you play your first gig at an old folks' home? It's an interesting choice.

Tom: Old folks like good music, too. What can I say, we have a growing gray fan base who are spreading the DOGZOMBIE word!

RW: What's in the future for DOGZOMBIES?

Tom: World domination, I think, and a sponsorship deal with a delicious biscuit company would be nice?

Delia rudely interrupts me.

Are you pretending to be interviewed?

"No," I say unconvincingly.

You are! SADDO. Ha! Ha!

Then she takes back her copy of **ROCK WEEKLY** and goes off

LAUGHING!

Ha! Ha! Ha! Ha!

I think the next song I write will be called
"My Sister is an IDIOT."
I have lots of ideas already.

Fresh from our SUCCESSFUL first-ever gig, me, Derek, and Norman are reliving the WHOLE event in school.

I say, "There were **loads** of people all cheering and clapping."

Which is *SORT* of true. ☺

I don't mention it was at the LEAFY GREEN OLD FOLKS' HOME either.

In class, everyone is settling down when Mrs. Mumble makes an announcement over the loudspeaker.

WILL TOM Gates and Norman Watson and Derek Fingle come to the School office TO See MR. KEEN . . .

Mr. Fullerman is looking at me with his "What have you been up to NOW?" stare as we leave.

Derek is already waiting outside the school office.

"What do you think Mr. Keen wants?" he asks me.

"Who knows. . . . Whatever it is, we're innocent," I say.

Norman's just happy to be out of lessons.

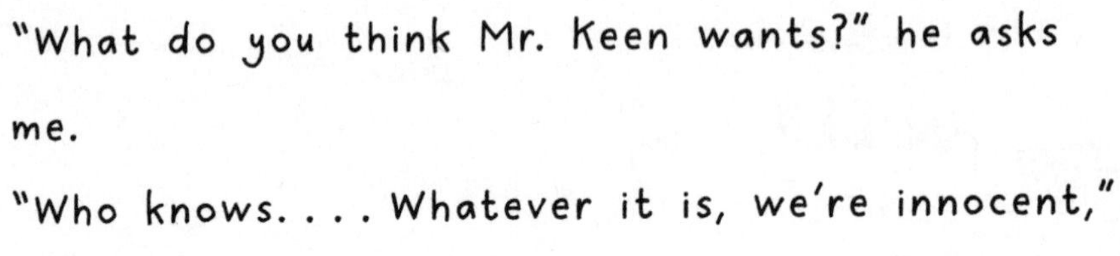

Turns out that Mr. Keen has had a phone call from the owner of the LEAFY GREEN OLD FOLKS' HOME saying how impressed they were with the band. Apparently we're "a credit to the school."

"Well done, all three of you,"

Mr. Keen says.

Then he goes and SPOILS EVERYTHING by telling us,

"You'll be even better in the school band now!"

Mr. Sprocket is running a special school band practice this lunchtime.

"I'll be showing some new parents around the school. It will be VERY impressive for them to see the band in action. Isn't that a good idea?"

(Eeeeeerrrr, NO!)

NOT the school band again.

Mr. Keen is DETERMINED to put us in the school band!

WHY? Looking at Derek, I can see he's not wild about the idea.

(Especially after last time.)

Norman doesn't seem to care because he's just spotted a spider walking up the wall.

I'm trying to think of YET another excuse to get OUT of this situation.

(Think! Mmmm . . . mmmmm . . . think! Mmmmmm . . .)

All kinds of ideas are going through my head.

Then it comes to me in a

FLASH!

"Yes, Tom."

"Would you mind if we DIDN'T play in the school band? We were SO RUBBISH at playing the recycled instruments last time. It was terrible. Everyone thought so."

"Oh . . . are you all sure?" Mr. Keen asks.

"Very," I say.

Derek and Norman are nodding, too.

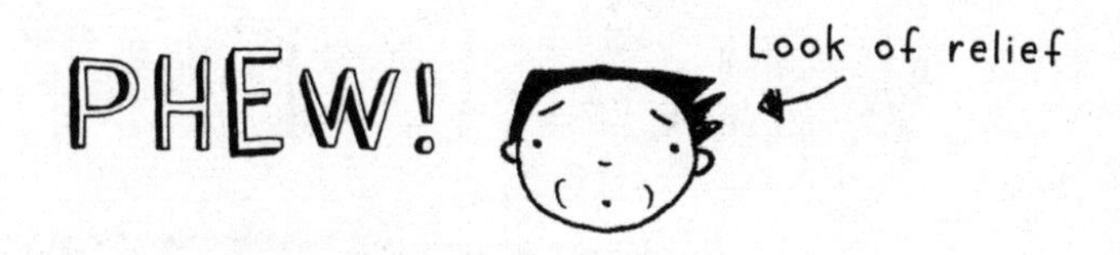

WHY didn't I think of saying that before?

And just like that, it's all sorted.

No more school band.

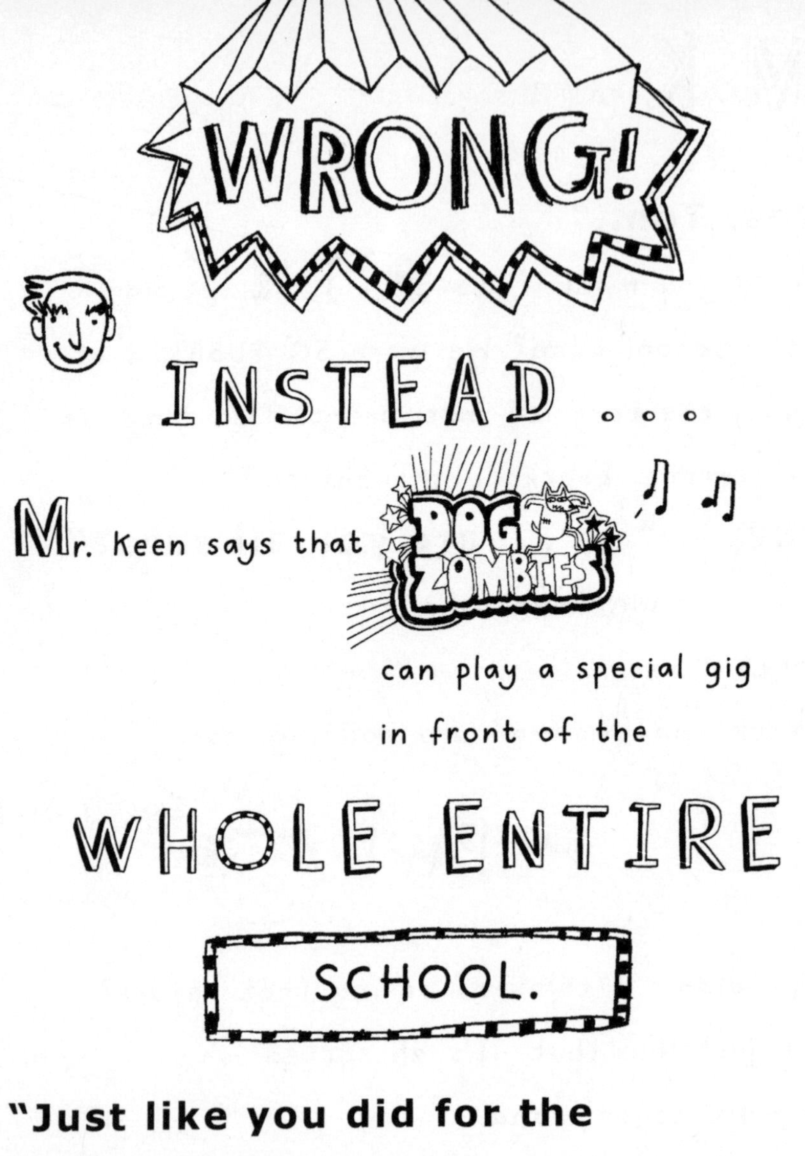

"Just like you did for the

LEAFY GREEN OLD FOLKS' HOME.

So, well done, Tom, for suggesting that," he adds.

(I didn't. . . . Groan.)

On the way back to class I tell Derek and Norman it will all be fine because Mr. Keen will probably forget about it. (He won't.)

"We're not ready to play in front of the school yet," I say.

We all agree on that.

Back in class.

I'm hoping Mr. Fullerman might have heard the news that Mr. Keen was VERY pleased with us (for a change). I might even get a bit of PRAISE?

No, nothing yet. Oh, well.

I get ready to join in the "class reading," which is a nice and easy lesson.

I've even remembered to sneak a copy of **ROCK WEEKLY** into my reading book just in case things get a bit dull. (Emergency reading, I call it.)

But Mr. Fullerman says I'm EXCUSED from class reading today because I still haven't handed in my REVIEW HOMEWORK.

"Have you, TOM?"

And if I don't finish it NOW I will have to do it at lunchtime in the library, with Miss Page keeping an eye on me.

"You don't want ANOTHER letter home, do you, Tom?"

"No, Mr. Fullerman."

"And no copying books on trees."

Groan.

Marcus is sniggering next to me. He says, "No gold stars for cheating," which is irritating.

OK. I'll do a REVIEW of DOGZOMBIES' first gig. It's fresh in my memory and shouldn't take long. I'll get it done before lunch.

I don't want to be stuck in the library, after all.

In the library,
I'm still finishing off
my homework.

I can hear people laughing and PLAYING outside and the school band practicing in the hall. Miss Page ➡ is keeping an EYE on me and a couple of other kids, too.

(At least I'm not in the school band anymore. . . . That's something.)

I'm hoping this review homework will be worth

SIX MERITS and 3 ☆ gold stars

Because right now Marcus is STILL in the lead on the CHART. Although I'm convinced he's been

CHEATING.

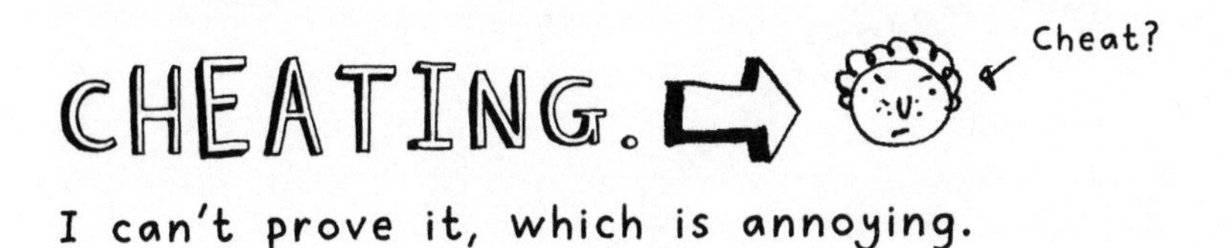

I can't prove it, which is annoying.

So I'm trying to get the last bit of my homework finished when I glance up and stare out the window. I notice something a bit

ODD.

From where I'm sitting in the library, I can see RIGHT INTO our CLASSROOM. SOMEONE is in there.

It doesn't look like Mr. Fullerman, Mr. Keen, or any of the teachers.

I can't see who it is. So I keep watching.

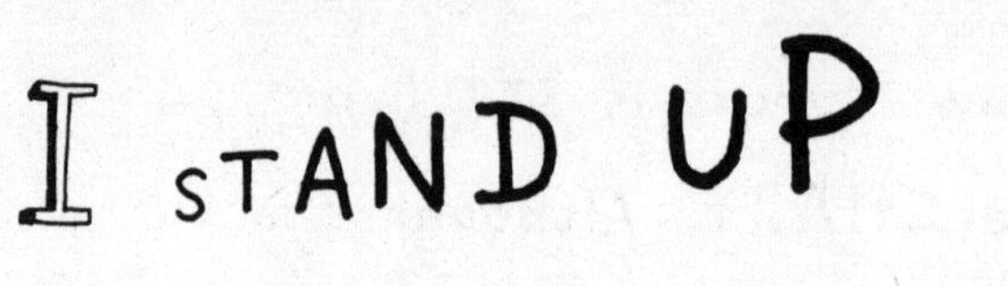

I STAND UP

for a closer look.

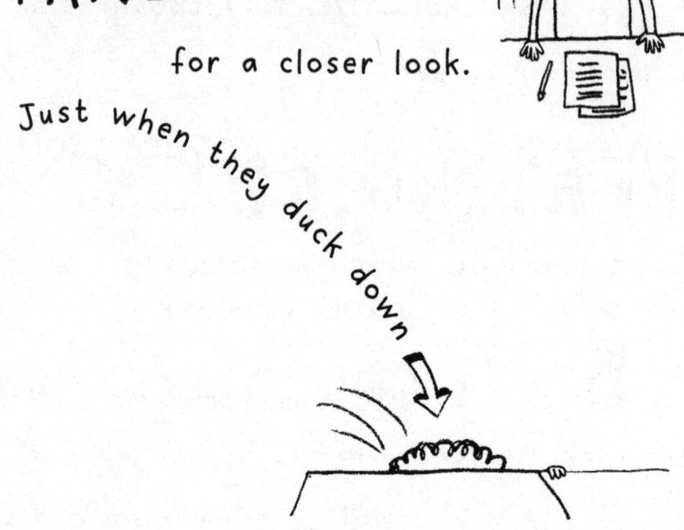

Just when they duck down

under the desks.

Which is VERY suspicious.

The school band is still playing, so it can't be any of them (or Mr. Sprocket).

Whoever it is has curly hair. I can see the top of their head moving closer

and closer

and closer

toward

This could be my chance to catch

a very sneaky

CHEAT.

Smug

I ask Miss Page if I can leave.

"Because Mr. Fullerman wants to check my FINISHED REVIEW HOMEWORK himself."

(Good thinking.)

Then I do super *FAST* walking to get to the classroom.

I'm SO nearly there when I

right into Mr. Keen. Who is busy showing the new parents around the school.

He asks me what I'm doing in school at lunch time?

I say EXTRA studying

(which is sort of true).

Then Mr. Keen tells the parents ALL about DOGZOMBIES

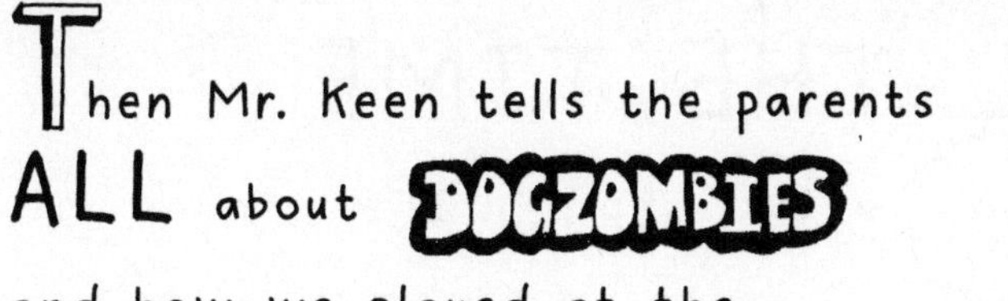

and how we played at the

LEAFY GREEN OLD FOLKS' HOME.

(He's going on a bit. Blah . . . blah, blah . . .)

I'm DESPERATE to get to the classroom!

Then, just when I think he's finished chatting . . .

Mr. Fullerman turns up!

And HE starts talking to the parents about **"the school field trip"** and what kind of work we do in class.

BLAH, BLAH, BLAH!

And ALL THE TIME

I'm thinking about who's in the classroom ADDING the GOLD STARS to the CHART!

When one of the PARENTS asks me,

What do YOU like about your school, Tom?

And THAT'S when I get one of my TOTAL BRAIN WAVES.

I say . . .

"I really like the

GOLD STAR AWARD CHART

because it encourages us to do well in class."

(Superb answer.)

"Sounds interesting," they say.

"How does it work?"

Then Mr. Keen suggests I might like to show them in my classroom.

And I say, "That's an EXCELLENT idea, follow me."

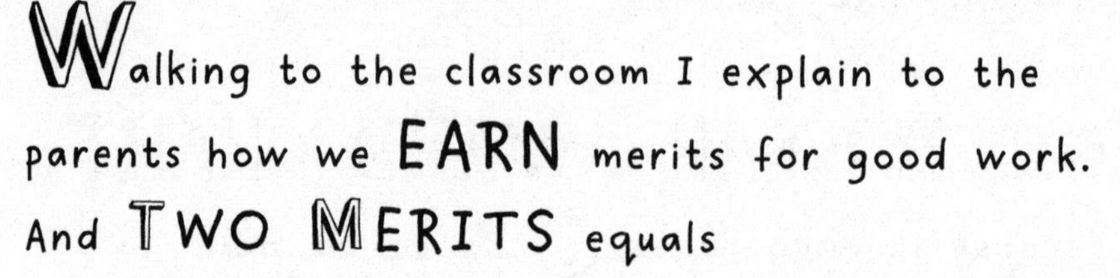

Walking to the classroom I explain to the parents how we EARN merits for good work. And TWO MERITS equals

ONE GOLD STAR

And the ONLY person who is allowed to give out the gold stars is MR. FULLERMAN.

"You are DEFINITELY NOT allowed to stick the stars on yourself,

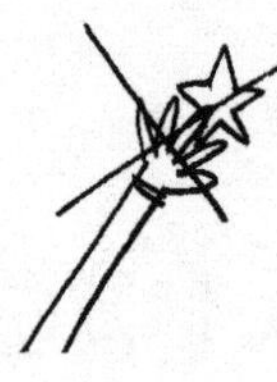

are you,
Mr. Fullerman?"
I say.

"No, Tom, that's my job. And I hand out prizes at the end of term to whoever has the most gold stars."

We're nearly outside the classroom now.

So I say,

"If Mr. Fullerman EVER caught someone adding their OWN stars to the chart, that would be cheating, wouldn't it, Mr. Fullerman?"

"Yes, Tom, it would be," he says.

Then I OPEN the classroom door, and just as I suspected . . .

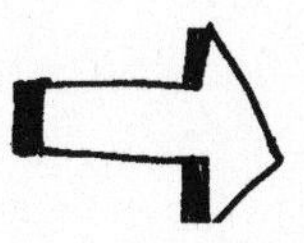

there's Marcus Meldrew with a whole packet of his own gold stars.

(He's SO busted.)

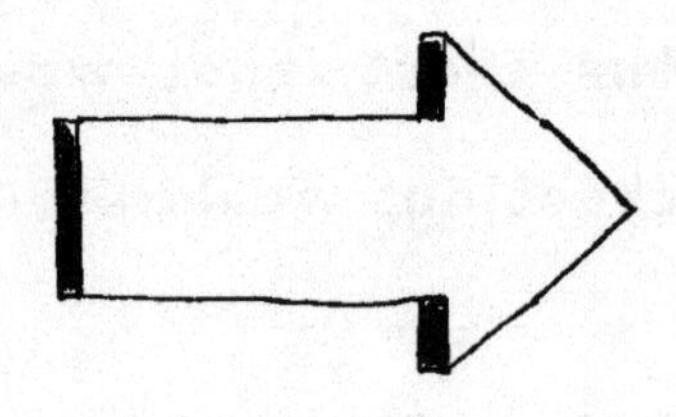

GOLD STAR AWARD CHART
CLASS 5F
MARK CLUMP
ROSS WHITE
BRAD GALLOWAY
SOLOMON STEWART
TOM GATES
PANSY BENNET
PAUL JOLLY
INDRANI HINDLE
LEROY LEWIS
FLORENCE MITCHELL
MA CUS MELDREW
JULIA MORTON
TREVOR PETERS
AMY PORTER
NORMAN WATSON
AMBER TULLEY GREEN

Dear Mr. and Mrs. Meldrew,

I am very disappointed to tell you that Marcus has been caught adding his own stars to the GOLD STAR AWARD CHART. In other words, he's been caught cheating.

Marcus will be missing playtimes for the next three days and helping Miss Page in the library as a punishment.

Along with writing an apology letter to me.

I hope Marcus has learned his lesson, as he is capable of earning his own stars without cheating.

Kind regards,

Mr. Fullerman

Class 5F Teacher

Due to Marcus CHEATING . . .

his stars have been removed.

from AMY PORTER (who's in the lead).

I need to get four merits (or more) for my REVIEW HOMEWORK on the DOGZOMBIES gig.

Mr. Fullerman has been taking AGES to mark my work.

When he does give it back to me he says there's been a bit of a problem.

WHAT NOW?

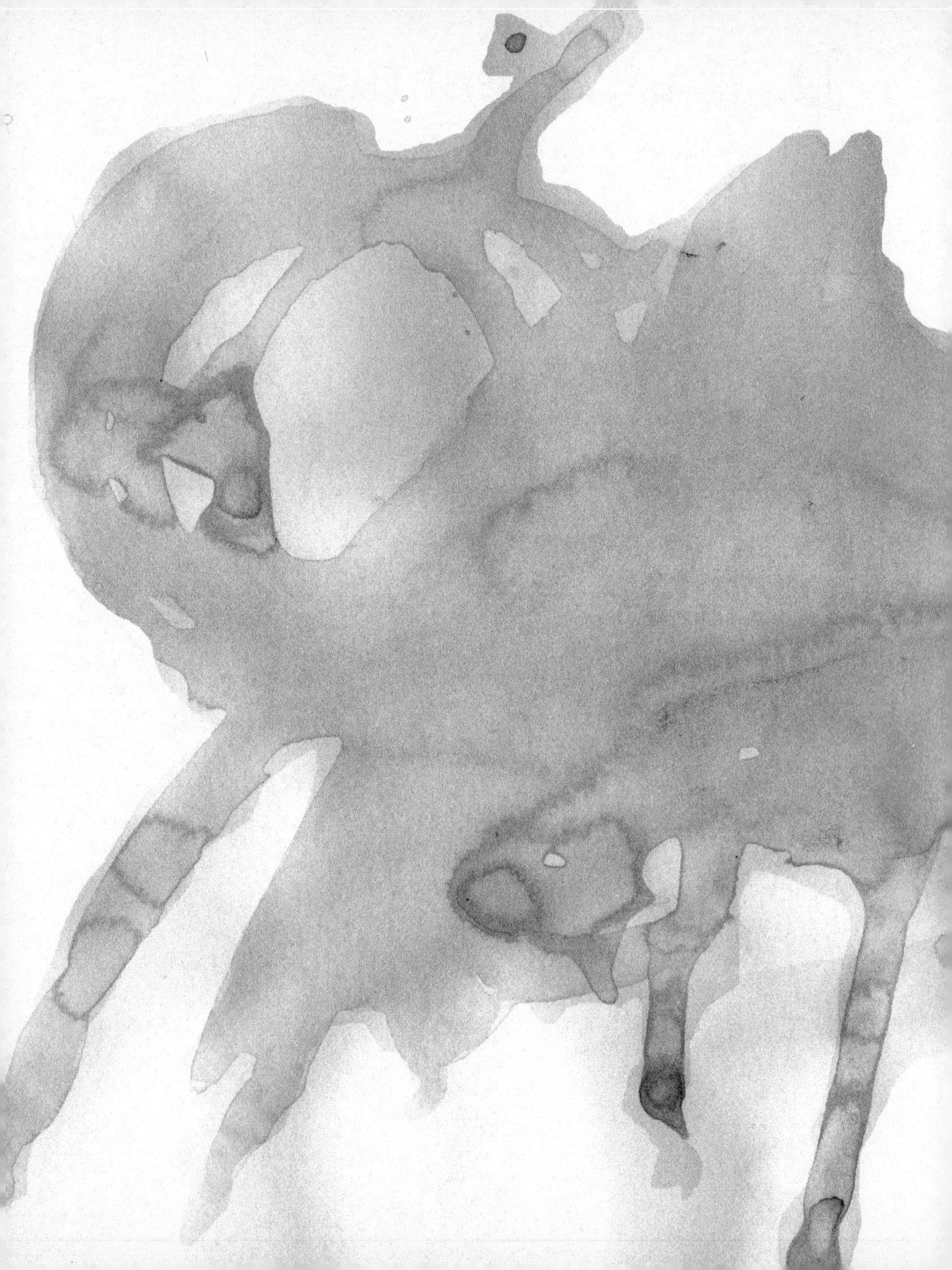

Sorry, Tom.

I had a bit of an accident with my coffee!

Luckily it missed your homework and I was able to read and mark it finally.

Please make sure you do homework on time in the future?

Mr. Fullerman

FIRST-EVER GIG

REVIEW HOMEWORK AGAIN.

(For the ~~SECOND~~ THIRD TIME)

By Tom Gates

If I were the lead singer of DUDE 3, I might be a tiny bit disappointed finding out the venue for the gig was THE LEAFY GREEN OLD FOLKS' HOME.

But for DOGZOMBIES' first gig it was excellent.

My granddad BOB arranged it all. (Thanks, Granddad.)

We had to carry a LOT of stuff into the home to set up.

Well . . . when I say "WE," I mean my dad, who was our roadie for the day.

Before we could get started we had to wait for the

to finish.

Then Dad wasn't allowed to use the BIG hammer he brought to put up our DOGZOMBIES banner.

Luckily the surgical tape worked just as well.

Granddad said,

"Everyone who lives here is coming to see you because they are all

"

But I'm not so sure that's true. Because outside there was a sign that said tea and biscuits and band playing.

I managed to STOP Norman from eating any biscuits before the gig started in case he went

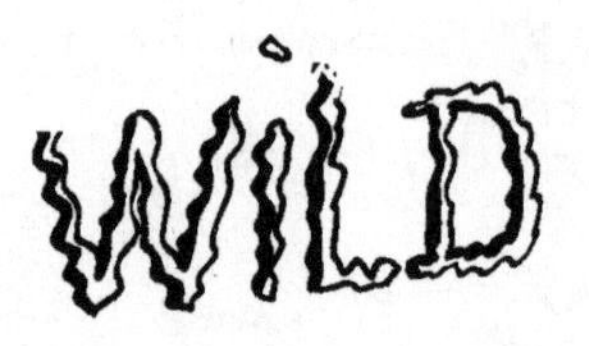

(again).

It took a LONG time for
everyone to get seated and comfortable.
And even longer for us to start
playing.
This was mostly because:
1. I completely forgot what
song we were starting with.
And we had to start again twice.
2. Norman accidentally knocked
over a cymbal, which made a
MAssivE
CRASH.

3. Some of the OLD FOLKS got a BIT of a

SHOCK from the noise and needed a top-up of tea and a biscuit to calm down.

4. Vera in the second row couldn't see

properly because **George's** head was in the way. So Dad had to help Vera to a better seat.

5. Finally . . . we were just about to get started when FRED wanted to know why we were called **DOGZOMBIES**.

Which was a good question and took a bit of explaining.

EVENTUALLY . . . we did start playing. "Delia's a WEIRDO" went down well. So did "WILD THING."

But the best song of all was "SMOKE ON THE WATER."

Because everyone joined in by tapping the sides of their teacups in time with the music.

Tap

The whole GIG went SO well that at the end we got a

STANDING OVATION . . .

Which is not easy to do
when most of the audience
is well over

The End

Six merits, Tom, and
THREE GOLD STARS.

WELL DONE!

Mr. Fullerman

HOORAY!
Oh, yes . . . see those
extra stars twinkling on
the award chart!
Excellent!

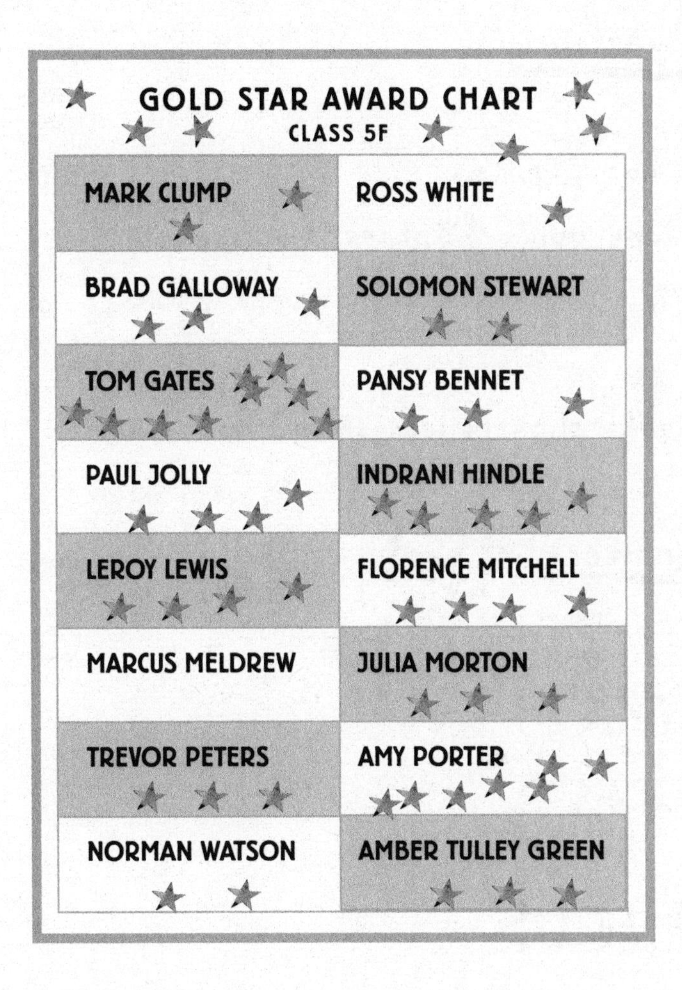
GOLD STAR AWARD CHART
CLASS 5F
MARK CLUMP
ROSS WHITE
BRAD GALLOWAY
SOLOMON STEWART
TOM GATES
PANSY BENNET
PAUL JOLLY
INDRANI HINDLE
LEROY LEWIS
FLORENCE MITCHELL
MARCUS MELDREW
JULIA MORTON
TREVOR PETERS
AMY PORTER
NORMAN WATSON
AMBER TULLEY GREEN

Question

What has Spots,

not many gold ☆ stars

(NOW),

and looks slightly less smug than usual?

Answer

MARCUS

(the cheater)

Finished reading
this book ALREADY?
You might like the same kind
of FUNNY stuff I do.
So check out my BLOG
www.theworldoftomgates.com

Tom Gates' Glossary

(Which means explanations for stuff that might sound a bit ODD.)

Ace: When something is GREAT ☺ or BRILLIANT.

Biscuits = cookies.

Bodge (or bodged): When I make a MESS of something or it get ruined (like this picture is BODGED now).

BONKERS = Crazy nuts!
Bogeys = BOOGERS.
Caramel wafers: Excellent biscuits (cookies) covered in chocolate with layers of caramel and wafer inside.
WAFERS
Crisps: Chips.
Crisps
Dodgy = something that's a bit ODD or wrong. Maybe slightly peculiar or not quite right. For instance: That apple looks a bit Dodgy.
That monster looks a bit dodgy.
(worm)

Fizzy drinks:

Pop or soda.

Fruit chews = candy.

Garden is a YARD.

Headmaster is a principal.

Lads: BOYS.

Lessons = the same as **CLASSES**.

LURGY is an imaginary (or real) DISEASE. Something NASTY you can catch or give to another person (like this).

MANKY means disgusting or revolting. For instance, this mint that rolled on the floor is manky.

(So is Rooster's fur.)

Mate = FRIEND

Derek (my best mate).

MERITS are special POINTS or STARS awarded by your teacher for excellent work.

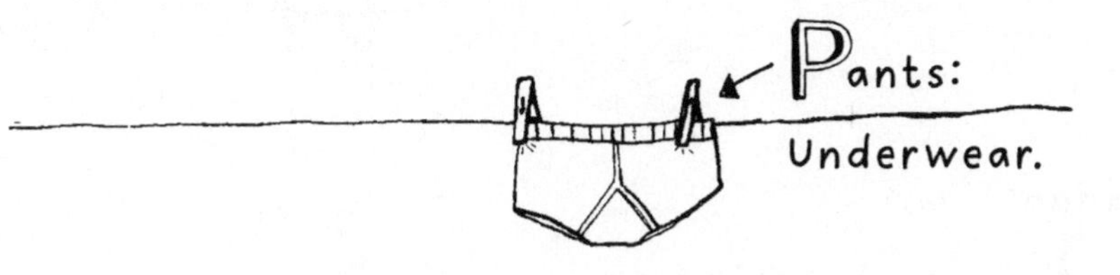

Pants: Underwear.

RANK: Unpleasant or GROSS (like Dad's running shoes).

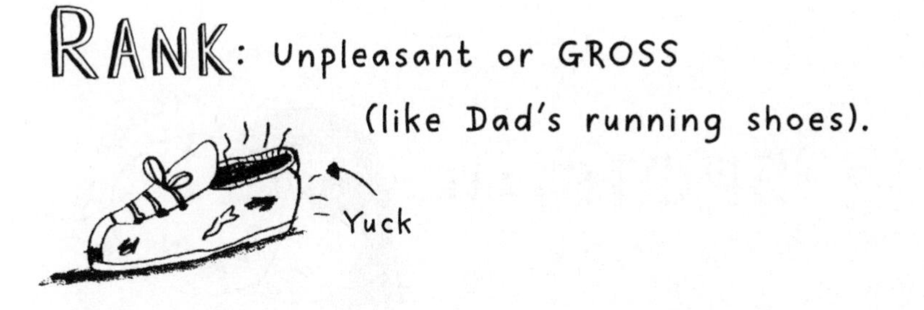

is the attendance book that the teacher would ✓ tick you off in, in the morning to make sure you're not LATE.

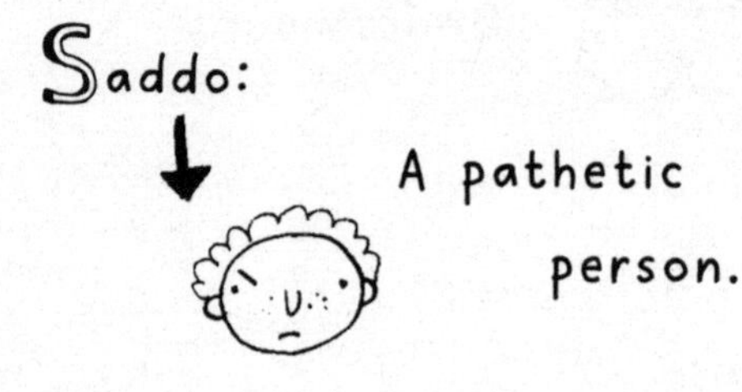

Tea towels = dish towels.

TELLY = TV.

When Liz was little, she loved to draw, paint, and make things. Her mom used to say she was very good at making a mess (which is still true today!).

She kept drawing and went to art school, where she earned a degree in graphic design. She worked as a designer and art director in the music industry, and her freelance work has appeared on a wide variety of products.

Liz is the author-illustrator of several picture books. Tom Gates is the first series of books she has written and illustrated for older children. They have won several prestigious awards, including the Roald Dahl Funny Prize, the Waterstones Children's Book Prize, and the Blue Peter Book Award. The books have been translated into thirty-six languages worldwide. Liz works in a nice cozy shed in her yard and lives in (mostly) sunny Brighton with her husband and three (not so little anymore) children. She doesn't have a pet but she does have lots of squirrels in the yard that eat everything in sight (including her tulip bulbs, which is annoying).

Coming soon!

Tom Gates: Everything's Amazing (Sort Of)

More doodles,
more DOGZOMBIES,
and, sadly, more Marcus.

Why don't you check out my new diary . . .

Every
Am

Long

hing's
zing
(sort of)
All my own work
Coming in Fall 2015
dog
The Brilliant World of
TOM GATES
By L. Pichon
TOM GATES
Everything's
AMAZING
By L. Pichon

Good stuff

I won a **MASSIVE** pack of pens for being (nearly) TOP of the Gold Star Chart AND a huge bar of chocolate (eaten).

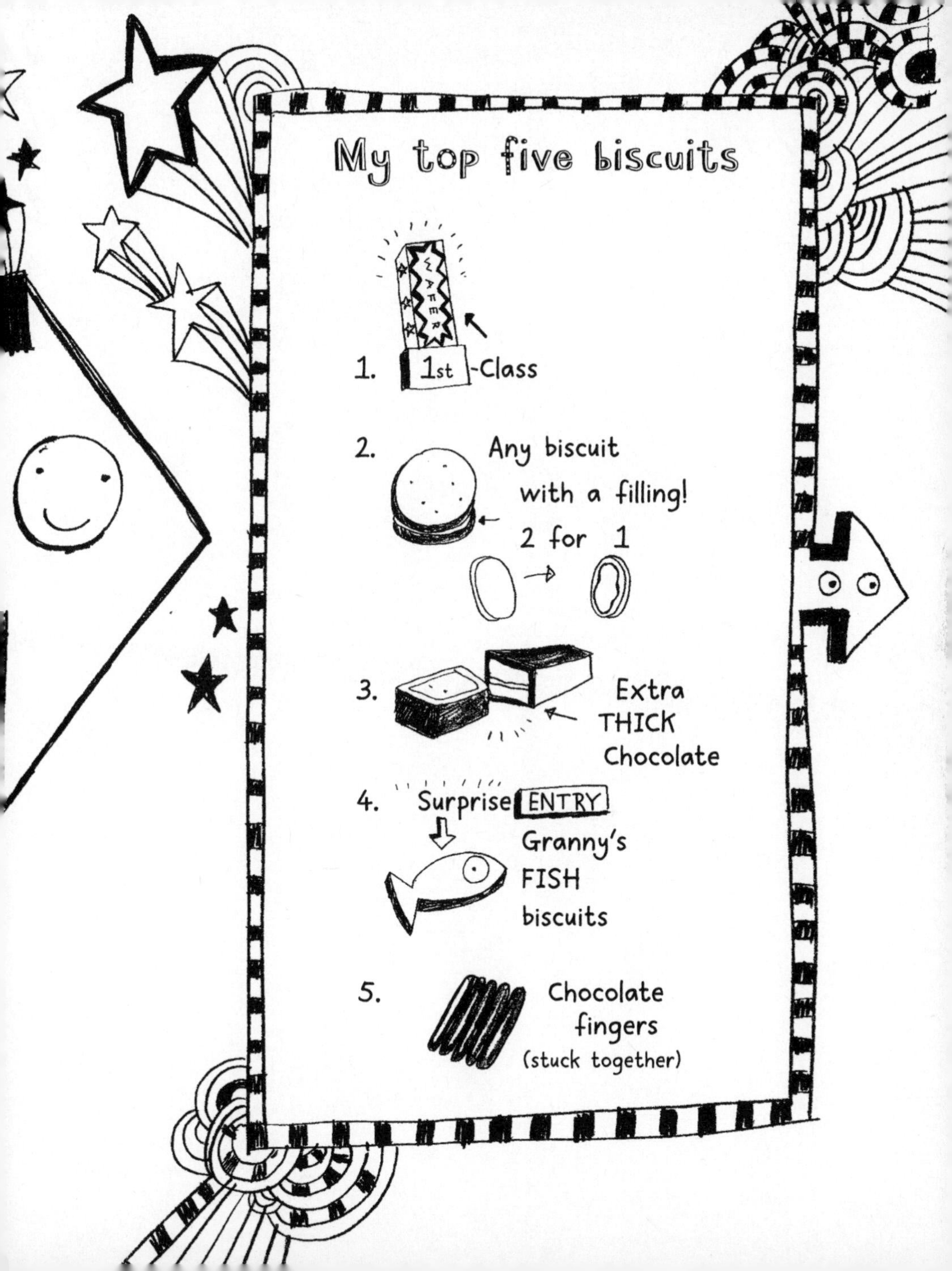
My top five biscuits
WAFER
1. 1st -Class
2. Any biscuit
with a filling!
2 for 1
3. Extra
THICK
Chocolate
4. Surprise ENTRY
Granny's
FISH
biscuits
5. Chocolate
fingers
(stuck together)